Table of Contents

Dark Days @ Crenshaw House

Chapter 1 Perfect Peace and Quiet

The Chicago skyline was peaceful and serene, but the streets below were fast-paced and hectic. An advancing thunderstorm threatened the beauty of the late summer day.

The Carltons, a black couple from Evanston, and the Cains, a white couple from Chicago, sat next to the window in Randalini's Restaurant overlooking the city. Shelli Carlton, a thirty-two-year-old medical researcher, leaned quietly over to Pat Cain, her co-worker and her best friend since college days, and whispered, "It's about time we plan our annual fall getaway."

"Yes, something we will never forget."

"This is our tenth anniversary of fall getaways. Let's do something special," responded Shelli.

James Harrison Carlton, a professor of history at Northwestern University, and Robert Cain, a Chicago stockbroker dealing in agricultural commodities, stopped their discussion about the Bulls' upcoming season to intercept their wives' conversation. "Did we hear something about THE getaway?" quipped Robert.

The two men met in the military. They served as MP's for most of their time in the service. When they finished their stints in the Army, they attended the same university where they met their wives. The racial difference in the couples had never been an issue. Their friendship continued after graduation into their professional lives.

"Oh, no, not more beach souvenir shops! I don't think I can look at another thing made out of shells," resisted James.

"And sunburns," added Robert.

"No, no, no, let's do something entirely different this year. We have done the usual tourist thing for the past nine years. This year let's get out of the crowds and out of the city. How about a country bed and breakfast?" suggested Pat.

"Check the internet while you are playing around at work," teased Robert who knew that they were all business when it came to their research.

"Playing around?—we are so stressed out by this research project we need a little R & R," Pat replied in disgust. The pair worked in DNA and cell memory research at a medical center in Chicago.

James gazed out the window just in time to see lightning strike one of the towers of the John Hancock Building. After a moment of reflection, he commented profoundly, "Isn't it strange how fate can deal such a devastating blow to one and yet leave another so close unscathed?"

James stopped the Navigator on a dime and parked in front of Robert and Pat. "Get in! We are ready for the open road and to leave the rat race behind."

Robert wedged in their last piece of luggage and remarked, "I am glad you have this SUV. We couldn't have packed everything into the ole 'Bimmer' or 'Beemer' as most people would say."

"Let's head for the expressway," James said in relief.

Leaving behind the tall buildings, exhaust fumes, noise, and litter of the city, the exit sign for I-57 came into view. The couples drove the interstate for a few hours and then decided to see the "real" countryside.

Within an hour the scenery had changed. The towns were exactly as described in the brochures, a throwback to the past—old buildings, authentic antiques, friendly local shopkeepers, and comfort food in small cafes and coffee shops. The laid back pace of the people and nostalgic atmosphere provided hours of enjoyable leisure. The couples were successful in their attempt to escape the fast pace of the city. Pastures, woods, picturesque barns, and colorful billboards punctuated the changing foliage of the beautiful autumn countryside.

James looked at his watch and said to Robert who liked his maps, "We need to get back on the interstate for a while if we are going to get to Arthur in time to have lunch and shop."

Robert agreed and gave James directions back to I-57. Several miles down the interstate, James finally spotted the sign for Arthur, Illinois. Robert, looking at the atlas, quickly noted, "We need Exit 203, State Highway 133 North."

"The sign said 'Arthur seven miles ahead'. We are getting close," responded James.

Ever the avid shopper, Pat grabbed her purse and exclaimed, "Get your checkbook and plastic ready; Arthur, here we come!"

the town. Eagle-eyed James spotted a picturesque shop hidden down a narrow street. The tourists walked eagerly toward a store named Unique Past Antique Shop. Each shopper, intrigued by a different section of the store, pursued his own interests. Shelli inspected an old tin-type camera while Pat made her way to the vintage clothing display. Robert was attracted to a glass-covered case where he spied some old Chicago Stock Exchange papers dating back to the 1800's. James moved quietly to the back of the store where the shopkeeper inquired, "Are you looking for something in particular?"

"No, but I'll recognize it when I see it!" James replied overwhelmed by the historic wealth contained within the walls of the old store. As he was about to turn down another aisle, his eyes focused on a top shelf. There sat a beautifully carved wooden box. As he reached up to retrieve it, his curiosity was sparked. He questioned the shopkeeper who was standing nearby, "How old is this?"

"I really don't know. I bought it at an estate sale only a few months ago. Many of the antique chests of drawers had handkerchief boxes to match. It is very possible a well-to-do man kept his handkerchiefs in it," informed the shopkeeper.

With great care, James removed the box from its resting place. He gently blew the dust from the carved wooden box lid and inspected it with an antique buff's eye for detail. James noticed a small cream-colored spot on the dark lid of the box. He removed a handkerchief from his back pocket and rubbed the wood softly revealing a craftsman's handiwork of inlaid ivory forming the initials "JCH". "This it IT," James gasped excitedly, "I knew I would know what I was looking for when I saw it. I must have this box; these are MY initials."

Shelli heard her husband's elated voice and made her way quickly to the back of the store. "What's all the excitement, James?"

"This is great, Shelli. My exact initials are on this box. It must be destiny!"

"I noticed it had a broken hinge when I bought it so I'll give you a good price," offered the shopkeeper.

"Wrap it up! This is my purchase for the day!" James exclaimed.

The couples enjoyed a quiet restful night to end an eventful day of travel. After a quick continental breakfast the next morning, they hurriedly packed looking forward to their final destination, Hickory Hill.

The eager travelers merged into the interstate traffic. Pat and Shelli harmonized, *"On the road again. . ."* and various other tunes from their past. The men good-naturedly teased them about their serenades.

"Speaking of 'On the road. . .' let's go off this boring interstate and take a more scenic route again. That was fun yesterday," suggested Pat.

"Great," Shelli agreed, "Maybe I can shoot some more pictures for our annual getaway photo journal."

Robert, now watching the GPS, said, "OK, we need to exit at Effingham on US 45 South."

"We might find some more little antique shops, but I won't find anything better than MY antique box," bragged James.

The miles and the hours seemed to fly by as the couples continued their journey southward. They sang, enjoyed the leisurely drive, and reminisced about their college days and friendship through the years.

Robert, the navigator of the journey, observed, "We need to take Highway 1 to Equality."

"Equality? I wonder what the history of that town's name is?" mused James.

"YOU are the history teacher," stated Robert. "Don't you know?"

"No," shrugged James, "but maybe we can find out at **Hickory Hill**."

Chapter 2 Journey Back in Time

"We must be getting closer to Hickory Hill. The landscape has changed. Yesterday we were in flat corn country; now we are in the hills," observed Robert.

The sun glistened on fall leaves and crumbling headstones as the friends passed an old cemetery located on one of the hills. James pointed to his left at the cemetery and said, "Notice the old, gnarled cedar trees in the graveyard. They are nature's living monuments that are 'ever green'. Man's decaying monuments are dark and lifeless, yet they seem to be in harmony," James noted philosophically.

"Oh, James, you and your profound statements. Lighten up! We should be getting closer to our vacation spot," teased Shelli.

"There's the road, Hickory Hill Lane. Turn right," directed Robert. "Look at the sign, 𝕳𝖎𝖈𝖐𝖔𝖗𝖞 𝕳𝖎𝖑𝖑, 𝖄𝖔𝖚𝖗 𝕻𝖊𝖆𝖈𝖊𝖋𝖚𝖑 𝖆𝖓𝖉 𝕾𝖊𝖗𝖊𝖓𝖊 𝕵𝖔𝖚𝖗𝖓𝖊𝖞 𝖙𝖔 𝖙𝖍𝖊 𝕻𝖆𝖘𝖙."

"Finally, we're here. Stop and let me take a picture from this view," said Shelli.

"Shelli, you picture nut, we are not even there yet," James' crooked smile betrayed his pretended annoyance at the idea. He was always eager to indulge his wife in her photography schemes and often suggested ideas for their growing gallery.

"I know, I know, but I want to remember this trip from beginning to end," she insisted.

The travelers hopped out of the vehicle. Shelli retrieved her tripod from the back and posed the other three with the house known as Hickory Hill in the background. She set the camera's timer and joined the others for the photo. The picturesque old house loomed over the beautiful fall countryside.

"How about changing places with me?" Shelli asked.

"Sure," Robert replied.

Picture taken, they drove up the winding drive to their destination. As they drew near the house, Pat exclaimed, "It's the perfect picture of a peaceful countryside inn."

Shelli, with a chill in her voice, gasped, "I just had the eeriest feeling that I have been here before."

"A bit of dé jà vu?" teased James, "Some of your 'cell memory' kicking in, perhaps?" James slipped his arm around his wife's shoulder as he kissed her lightly on the cheek.

Pat quickly jumped in the conversation and added, "Now remember what we said—no shop talk! We are here to get away from it all."

After parking, the couples unloaded the Navigator and with luggage in hand, they ascended the steps to the main floor porch. "The brochure mailed to us says it was built in 1834 and completed in 1838. Just think of all the history this house has seen. You know the old saying, 'If walls could talk, what stories they could tell'," James remarked deep in thought.

"Welcome to Hickory Hill," regaled a cheerful voice as the door opened to the old country inn. The couples walked into a beautifully decorated hall. "Let's get you registered, and we'll give you a tour of the house. Please step into the Lincoln Room. We are using this room while part of the first floor is under restoration," invited the innkeeper.

"The Lincoln Room?" Pat and Shelli both asked simultaneously.

"Yes, that is part of the folklore of this house. Lincoln was supposed to have stayed in this room while visiting the owner and politicking in Southern Illinois."

They walked up to an ornately carved oak bar serving as a check-in counter. James gently rubbed his hand along the smooth wood grain and asked admiringly, "Is this piece original to the house?"

"Oh, no, I purchased this in Marion, Illinois. It was used as a bar in an old saloon converted to a restaurant. Supposedly, it was on a steamboat that ran aground near Ste. Genevieve, Missouri. It had to be removed to lighten the load and was carried by wagon to Marion. I thought it would be a great addition to the old inn."

As the innkeeper turned the register back toward himself, he read, "Oh, yes, the Cains and the Carltons. I remember your e-mail reservations gave your home address as Chicago." James turned toward the others and introduced Shelli, Pat, Robert, and then himself.

"Welcome to your serene getaway. It will be a step back in time for you 'city folks'. We are the DeCheins. I'm Nick and my wife, Carla, is in the kitchen preparing the evening meal. We are happy to have you visit. Let's get you settled. We are expecting other guests, but you are the first to arrive. You may choose your rooms if you like. The second floor is newly decorated. Some of the furnishing were found on the grounds and restored."

"Welcome, I hope you are hungry; dinner will be ready shortly," Carla added as she joined them.

Robert and Pat promptly chose a bedroom with a brass bed at the front of the house overlooking the beautiful fall colors of the Saline River Valley. James and Shelli continued browsing to find just the right room. As James stuck his head in the last bedroom, he excitedly announced, "Let's stay in this room; I love the four poster bed. Look at the pineapples carved into the large posts. You know the story of the pineapple don't you,

Shelli?" Without pausing to let her answer, he continued, "The pineapple was a symbol of hospitality for sea captains in the 1700's and 1800's. When they had been away from home for a while in the tropics, they would bring back pineapples and display one in front of their houses when they were ready to receive guests."

Shelli looked at Nick and asked, "Can you tell he's a history professor?"

Shelli peered out the window and remarked, "Look at this breathtaking view and the old barn in the distance. It will be a great addition to my 'shutter bug' album."

"It *is* very picturesque," agreed Nick. "You also have a view of the old beech tree. It was brought as a tiny cutting from Washington's grave at Mount Vernon and planted when Hickory Hill was built."

"What other tidbits of information do you have about this place?" inquired James.

"I'll share what I know later when you get settled in," Nick promised.

As Shelli was unpacking, James climbed into the center of the four poster bed. He stretched out spread eagle looking all around the room. As he propped up on one elbow, he commented, "I could get used to this, Shelli, my dear."

"James Harrison Carlton, get off that bed," Shelli responded teasingly. James reached up and pulled his wife down next to him on the bed. He stroked the side of her face gently with the back of his fingers and kissed her neck lovingly.

"Come on, we have to meet Robert and Pat downstairs for our tour and dinner," Shelli said as she pulled her reluctant husband to his feet.

"Maybe we can find out more about the house from. . .uh. . .uh. . .what's their name?" inquired James.

"The DeCheins," replied Shelli as she was opening the door to leave.

"Right, the DeCheins."

As they started to descend the elegantly restored staircase, James offered his arm to Shelli with a playful smile and said, "May I escort you, Miss Scarlett?"

"Why, I would be honored, Mr. Rhett," she quickly replied joining in the frivolity of the moment.

Robert, Pat, and the innkeeper, waiting at the bottom of the stairs, noticed the couple's smirky grins. Robert inquired quickly, "What's so funny with you two? Reliving a scene from *Gone With the Wind*?"

"Just a little 'off color' humor, I guess."

"Are you ready for the tour?" asked Nick.

At that moment the couples' memories clicked, and the foursome burst out with the lyric: "A three hour tour..."

Nick, a little startled by the outburst, smiled and began his spiel. "You've seen the Lincoln Room. If you'll come out on the front porch, I'll start the official tour guide speech," he invited his guests. Once outside, Nick continued, "The house was built in the Greek Revival style. Construction on this house began in 1834 and was completed in 1838. I'm sure you read that in the brochure. We know the date is correct. When we were renovating, our contractor checked the foundation for soundness and discovered the date 1834 on the foundation stones. We hired a specialist in antique home renovation; he said he had never seen anything like the huge sills that looked like they were hand-hewn out of single trees."

As they descended the steps to admire the graceful porch, James inspected the underpinning more closely and observed, "It looks like this is made from hand-pegged framing lumber."

"Yes, that's another discovery the contractor made," confirmed Nick.

As the group walked out into the yard their eyes swept upward past the two large colonnaded porches and rested on a large window located in the center of the third story eave. "Our rooms are on the second floor. What's on the third?" inquired Shelli.

The group continued around the house as Nick replied, "There are two rooms on the front we don't use; the rest is sealed off. We hope to renovate more as our business grows, but right now we haven't done much work in that area."

Continuing around to the back of the house, Pat waved a hand toward the outline of something that had been removed. "It looks like there used to be big doors here. Why were they sealed, and why were there big doors there in the first place?"

"That's another mystery. Now our dining room is there," informed Nick.

"Speaking of dining rooms," Robert jumped in the conversation. "Isn't it about time for dinner? I've been looking forward to some great country 'cuisine'."

Shelli noticed the beautiful sunset as the group headed around the west side of the house. The blood red sun was sinking behind the black outline of the trees in the distance. "Look at the finger like rays trying to escape from the dark clouds. It's beautiful yet somehow ominous. Let me get my camera out of its case and capture this scene. It will make a great picture."

"Come on, Shelli," teased James, "the sun will set again tomorrow."

"Yes, but I'll never see *this* sunset again," his wife insisted.

Shelli snapped a couple of quick shots; then once inside the house, Nick wound up the tour. "Originally there were six rooms on the first two floors with ceilings twelve feet high. When we decided to lower the ceilings to conserve heat, we discovered the original ceilings were heavily plastered with mortar made from sand and horsehair."

"Hair?" gasped the two women.

"Yes, hair! It was a common practice in those days to use hair in building materials and in decorative pieces—both horse and human. There's one of those pieces in the Lincoln Room. Be sure to look at it," suggested the innkeeper.

After dinner, the couples retired to their own rooms. As soon as James and Shelli closed their door, he remembered the carved handkerchief box purchased the day before in the antique shop. I'm going down and get my 'purchase of the century'!"

Shelli teased, "Oh, you and your purchases. You'd think you had found the *Dead Sea Scrolls*."

"Well, you never know," he said confidently as he closed the door behind him.

James wandered into the crisp fall night anxious to inspect his antique purchase. The full moon shone brightly as James stepped energetically through dry fall leaves glistening with the first light frost of the season. Once the back hatch of the Navigator was up, he meticulously searched for his purchase. "Where in the heck is that box? Those women bought all this junk," he quipped as he continued the search for the only worthwhile purchase in his opinion. "Bingo! There you are!" he exclaimed as he shoved aside several packages to expose a large white paper bag with **Unique Past Antique Shop, Arthur, Illinois,** written in bold black letters.

James bounded up the front steps two at a time in his hurry to escape the night air and investigate his new "treasure". As he reached to open the front door, someone startled the preoccupied professor.

"I almost locked you out," chuckled Nick. Noticing the large package, he commented, "I see you folks found Arthur on your way down. They have some great antique shops, don't they? We bought several pieces for the house there. Don't forget breakfast; we start serving at 8 a.m. sharp!" Nick reminded his guest as James headed for the stairs.

The room was dimly lit as James entered. Immediately, he noticed the soft glow of the candles and his wife's shapely silhouette at the east window. As she turned to him, she softly whispered, "I was just admiring the beautiful view."

"I was just admiring the beautiful view, too," he gently replied as he pulled her close to him. Shelli's warm, freshly showered body pressed softly against James's more firm masculine physique. Her scent brought back vivid memories of the first time their bodies touched. James closed his eyes as the touch of Shelli's fingers made feather like strokes on the back of his neck. He responded to her touch and took Shelli's face in his strong but gentle hands and kissed her warm, moist lips. Each felt the tenderness of the moment but gave in to the hours and miles of the trip that stole the opportunity of this intimate fragment of time.

Shelli gently reminded him, "We've had a long day, and we need to get some rest."

James quietly kissed her lovingly on the neck. Then he moved slowly toward the en suite to ready himself for bed and what he hoped would be a good night's rest. "You go on to sleep; I won't be long," James said with a sigh. After his quick shower, he slipped quietly into bed trying not to disturb his already sleeping wife.

James glanced over and saw the package from Arthur; he slid out of bed waking his wife. "James, come to bed.

You can examine your antique box tomorrow," she said sleepily.

"Go back to sleep. I won't be long."

James stepped quietly toward the table and freed the box from its additional binding of paper and twine. As he ran his hand over the smooth, carved surface, he gently opened the box taking care not to break the other hinge. Inside the box, the soft light of the room revealed two yellowed handkerchiefs embroidered with delicate stitches, several antique buttons, and an old newspaper clipping.

After careful examination, James decided the inside depth of the box was not as great as the depth of the entire box. Upon further inspection, James realized it had a false bottom. A little tampering revealed a corner loose enough to be lifted with the help of his pocket knife. He carefully removed the old wooden bottom, and the dim light of the room exposed a dusty, time-worn leather bound book. James slowly and carefully exhumed the old volume from its hiding place. He gasped as beads of perspiration appeared on his forehead at the thought of unlocking secrets from the past.

Nervously, James felt the dry, cracked cover. "Time has not been kind to you—my new found treasure," the historian mumbled softly to himself. A shadow of a smile appeared as he surprised himself with his own profoundness.

Needing more light, he quietly moved closer to the antique Tiffany reading lamp. It was time for the old book to relinquish its long-kept secrets. "It's a journal!" he stifled a yell not wishing to wake his sleeping wife.

Too excited to read silently, James began reading barely above a whisper.

The journal began. . .

March 17, 1871

The howlin March wind woke me from a restless sleep. It is not the wind alone that bothers me. As I set here with pen in hand writin by my Mas old oil lamp I feel like I need to writ about things that have filled more than threescore and ten years of my life. I was born in 1797 in North Carolina. My ma and pa named me John Hart Crenshaw. My pa William Crenshaw moved our family west to New Madrid in 1808 with big dreams of gittin rich. The truth was that we was por dirt farmers.

He put the reins of a team of mules in my hands at an early age so I did not git much book learnin. At times I can still feel my blistered hands and feet and smell the fresh turned ground. The rich black dirt was an unforgivin master and so was my Pa. The acres of cotton had to be planted hoed and picked. In the fall of the year I drug the gunny sack down the long rows with my fingers bleedin and swelled from pricks of the dried cotton bolls. I swore that one day I would be the master.

April 9, 1871

In the early dark hours of December 18 1811 I woke up to a loud noise soundin like thunder but there was no lighten! Our cabin was black as pitch. The room begin to shake like the earth was about to swaller it up. The few things that Ma had in the room were throwed down to the dirt floor. It shook Pa out of bed and he got up and tried to light this here oil lamp that I am writin by tonight. He finally found some matches in the shaken house and lit the lamp but the light was so dim the room was still to dark to see much.

Days after the shaken stoped Pa moved us north to Gallatin County Illinois cause he feared another earth shaken might tear up our house agin. Not long after movin to Illinois Pas dreams of gitten to be a rich landowner died with him. The job of takin care of Ma and six brothers and sisters got to be my burden to bear. Like my seein other memorys of my bein a youngun have become dim with the passin years. Maybe my seein will be better tomorrow if I can rest my eyes tonight without the nightmares that haunt me.

March 25, 1871

By my 18 birthday I figured to git out of dirt farmin and find a better way to take care of my family. I got me a job at the salt works over at Equality but that work was not easy. My job was to draw water and put it into vats. I had to stoke the fires under those vats so we could boil down the water and git the salt that was left behind. The work was hard and hot. Some of them men and boys could not stand up to the backbreakin work and some of them wouldnt work. Sometimes I had to work right next to slaves. As my muscles got stronger with this backbreaking work so did my will to git myself up out of bein por and git rich and powerful. Not like my Pa I would do whatever need be to make my dream come true. That nigger work was for other men—not me. I noed that in my heart. In 1817 at the age of twenty I married Sina Taylor and we set up housekeepin. I noed I had to work harder. In a few years I got a better job than drawin water for the boilin kettles. That started a long path to what I am today.

June 1, 1871

As I worked longside some of the old timers I learnt that years before the red man had boiled the salt water for their needs. When the white men came they started makin money from the salt.

It helped me when the red men moved west. In 1812 Congress gave six square miles of land to be leased. Salt was sellin for $5 a bushel. The settlers moving west needed it to keep food from spoilin. River keelboats took the salt to sell in places a long way from here.

The need for pure white salt became the beginnin of my wealth. I finally was able to lease the salt works by learnin the governments dealins from the overseer. Lucky for me the state of Illinois wrote in their law something that let me use rented slaves and Illinois was a free state. I had fokes over in Livingston County acrost the river in Kaintucky who rented me their slaves durin the winter after their crops was in. Those fools thought they were makin a good deal with me. I did better than that. I had men workin for me who caught runaways comin acrost the river. I worked some of em in my salt works and sold some of em back to plantation owners in the south. Those slaves thought they would be able to buy their freedom but most of em never escaped me. I took care of em jest like I did my cattle. I gave em food and a roof over their heads.

Shadows of sunlight were dancing on the table and floor of the room when James crawled into the bed with his sleeping wife. Daylight and a gentle fall breeze

drifted through the tiny cracks in the windows and
through the lace curtains of the old inn displaying a
fanciful pattern on the wood floor. Thoughts danced in
James' head in the same darting fashion. Visions of the
journal stole the sleep from his weary body. The
hopelessness, the inhumanity, and the degradation
flooded his body and soul until he finally fell into a fitful
sleep.

James' short slumber was interrupted by the gentle
touch of his wife's hand. "It's almost breakfast time,"
Shelli sighed. "I've already had my shower; the
bathroom is all yours."

James dragged himself slowly into the bathroom. As
steam shrouded the room, he caught the faint scent of
lavender from the candle Shelli had thoughtfully left lit.
In spite of the normally relaxing fragrance of lavender
and the soothing steaminess of the shower, James was
still tense. His thoughts reverted to the words of the old

journal which had earlier vividly described the steam of the boiling salt kettles.

He was abruptly shaken back to the present by Shelli's voice. "Honey, Robert and Pat are waiting. We have a lot of exploring to do today." James quickly toweled off and slipped into some comfortable clothes and shoes.

Chapter 3 Evil Deeds in the Old Journal

As James descended the oak staircase, the smell of freshly brewed coffee permeated the air. He took a deep breath as his taste buds were stimulated by the breakfast aromas. James bounded down two steps at a time and inquired, "What's for breakfast? I'm starved!"

Shelli's beautiful smile met him at the doorway of the inn's breakfast room. Holding her husband's chin in her hand, Shelli replied, "Wait until you see all of these goodies!"

The warm sun of the fall morning streamed through the inn's old windows. Sunlight glistened with tiny particles captured by the old house. As the couple joined their friends and hosts for the beginning of a new day, the atmosphere of the dining area was comfortable and cozy. Nick and Carla had prepared a feast. "We thought you might enjoy some of our 'country living' specialties," Carla said with a quiet, meek voice.

Nick added, "Come on in and get started on this spread!"

"I've never seen such a breakfast!" Robert exclaimed with a voice of experience for culinary delights.

"We have country ham and biscuits, homemade pancakes with maple or fresh blueberry syrup, hash brown casserole, and sausage balls. You'll love those," Nick boasted to Robert.

"We have several kinds of fresh fruit and juices too. Oh, and don't forget some of my homemade strawberry and blackberry jams. I picked the blackberries myself on the property," Carla informed them. "They are wonderful on hot, buttered, homemade biscuits!"

The men piled their plates high with some of each of the many choices. "We want to sample everything," Robert said enthusiastically. "We have several things to see and do today, so we need a boost!"

Pat and Shelli took time to observe and ask questions about each specialty's unique preparation and presentation. "Carla, your buffet presents the food beautifully," Pat commented.

Each person found a seat at the large, round oak table. They were absorbed with each dish and the leisurely conversation of the morning. James questioned Nick,

"Do you mind if I ask a blessing for the food?"

Nick gave a quick glance to Carla and then replied, "Of course not, go right ahead, James."

After saying grace, the three couples enjoyed the wonderful tastes and aromas in the country inn breakfast area. The conversation varied from the Chicago drive, other guests' arrivals, and plans for the day as well as the stopover in Arthur.

During the conversation, James excitedly mentioned his unique purchase from Thursday. "I bought a beautiful, old, carved, wooden box in Arthur!" James said proudly. He could barely hold back the details of last night's historical discovery, but he restrained himself until the time seemed just right.

After the couples finished eating, the conversation turned back to the plans for the day. Nick tuned in to the couples' discussion. He added a suggestion, "We have a beautiful, self-guided trail on the property that may interest you. It meanders down by the Saline River and ends below the house."

Shelli reminded the group, "Remember the brochure we picked up at the rest area about the Garden of the Gods? We said we didn't want to miss that short trip."

Pat agreed, "OK, let's do the nature trail here first. Then we can drive over to the Garden of the Gods. We can pick up picnic supplies at a local grocery."

Carla volunteered eagerly, "Oh, no, I won't hear of it. I'll pack a nice picnic lunch for the four of you and have it ready when you return from the nature trail excursion."

Pat exclaimed, "That's fantastic! Shelli, grab your camera, and let's get started. I want to work up an appetite for lunch. Let's meet on the front porch in ten minutes."

The yellows, oranges, and reds of the native hardwoods against the bright blue fall sky of Southern Illinois were an artist's delight. The vivid colors and crisp air energized the four friends.   Each couple walked

hand in hand following the well-kept, self-guided trail.

The foursome read many of the handcrafted informative

signs on the trail leading to the river.   The last sign,

closest to the water, struck a chord in James' memory.

He quickly glanced at the sign again and read aloud,

"Saline River-Saline Springs-Water Source for ancient

salt works first used by Native Americans and later used

to produce salt for frontier pioneers."   Glancing up

quickly, his voice quivered as he explained, "I read about

the salt works in the old journal last night."

"What old journal?" Shelli asked.

"Remember the old wooden box I bought on the way

down?"

"The one with your initials on it?" Robert quizzed.

"Yes, after we went upstairs last night, I came back

down and 'rescued' it from all the other purchases and

brought it back to our room.   After Shelli and I went to

bed, my curiosity got the best of me. I had to inspect its contents. I remembered the shopkeeper's attention to the broken hinge. I opened it carefully and there was nothing there except two cotton handkerchiefs, some buttons, and a newspaper clipping. But, I thought something was odd about the box."

Robert inquired, "What could be odd about a wooden box?"

"I noticed the box was deeper on the outside than it was inside," James explained.

"So?" chimed in Pat. "What was so strange about that?"

James continued, "I discovered it had a false bottom! I used my pocketknife to pry up what I had thought was the bottom..."

"What was in it-- money, jewels, a map?" facetiously interrupted Shelli.

"I found an old journal," James informed the captivated group.

"How old is this journal? Was it a business ledger? Did it contain any deeds or contracts?" business-minded Robert questioned.

"The first entry was dated March 17, 1871. It was written by a man named John Hart Crenshaw who worked in and eventually owned a salt work," James replied.

"Was that all there was to the journal?" Shelli asked.

"I didn't read all of it last night, but this sign reminded me of that part of the journal. Oh, just forget it. Let's go on with our nature walk. We need to pick up our lunches and head for the Garden of the Gods." The other three shrugged their shoulders. They briskly finished their walk and ventured on to their next destination.

Back at the inn, the foursome hurried up the steps to the large front porch. James turned the brass doorknob. As the door made an eerie creaking noise, Carla's timid voice responded to the sound and shyly muttered, "You folks, come on in. I have your lunches ready."

Robert answered excitedly, "Great, I'm hungry already. What's in it?"

Pat quickly replied, "How can you be hungry after that huge breakfast? It'll be great whatever it is."

The friends freshened up, packed their lunches in the SUV, and started on the short journey to the Garden of the Gods. The drive on Highway 1 was pleasant. The sun was bright and the temperature was in the 60's. The colorful array of trees and rock formations made the trip enjoyable for the city dwellers.

Robert found the brochure Pat had picked up at a rest stop's information booth. He scanned the brochure and reported some of the most interesting points, "Listen to this---Welcome to scenic Garden of the Gods Country. It's located between the Ohio and Mississippi Rivers in the Shawnee National Forest. It drew early travelers to settle on the mighty Ohio with its lush forests. It has scenic roads along the Ohio River and through rolling hills with mysterious hollows, rocky bluffs, unique rock formations, caves, volcanic upthrusts, and hardwood forests. The Wisconsin glaciation stopped short of these hills preserving these unique geological characteristics."

He continued, "Early visitors included Tecumseh—he was a famous Native American wasn't he, Professor Carlton? Others were Lewis and Clark, the famous explorers, and Davy Crockett. Hey, listen to this--river pirates, counterfeiters, and slave traders also used this area. It says here that the oldest bank, some of the oldest churches, and the oldest hotel still in use are located in this vicinity."

"The hotel might be a neat place to spend a night,"

suggested Pat.

Robert continued his description from the brochure, "The Shawnee Hills are about 320 million years old and were originally covered by a giant inland sea. Melting water from glaciers eroded the limestone and sandstone rocks shaped by eons of time and wind. These elements created the unusual formations in the Garden of the Gods such as Camel Rock, Anvil Rock, and Devil's Smokestack."

"Boy, Robert, that was a lot of information. I can't wait to walk some of the trails and see Camel Rock," James said eagerly.

"And Devil's Smokestack too," Shelli added.

Robert reminded them, "Don't forget about our lunches. Let's find a nice quiet spot on one of the wooded trails overlooking a 'mysterious hollow'."

James, more interested in history than eating, asked, "What did you say about slave-trading? We will have to find out more about that."

The SUV traveled up the narrow, crooked road to the parking area and the couples' anticipation grew. "We're here!" exclaimed Robert. "Let's get the lunches!"

"Lunches?" James questioned. "Can't I find a parking space first?"

After her husband had parked, Shelli instructed, "You guys, get the lunches and the drinks, and Pat and I will grab a couple of blankets. I'll get my camera. The brochure sounded like there will be many photo ops here."

The excited duos, with lunches and other hiking "necessities" in hand, walked leisurely up the winding trail. At the top of the hill above the parking area, Pat spotted the trail sign "To Camel Rock". Robert, with his voracious appetite, responded to Pat's find with, "That sounds like a great spot for lunch."

James laughed, "Let's feed 'Brontosaurus Robert' so we can continue our exploration. I want to see if we can find any more information about the slave trade that was once in this area."

The girls walked on ahead, spotted Camel Rock, and motioned for their husbands. They found a flat area with a good view of the unique rock formation, spread the blankets, and eagerly opened Carla's mysterious lunch parcel with culinary anticipation. Robert quizzed eagerly, "What did 'Miss Carla' prepare for us today?" As he carefully delved into the picnic basket, he began answering his own question. "We have several different varieties of cheeses and fruit, olives, pickles, sesame crackers, Reuben sandwiches, and chocolate layer cake for dessert! Yum! Who wants some bottled water?"

The couples enjoyed their early afternoon meal while they appreciated the panoramic view of Camel Rock and nature's autumnal palette. After lunch the couples continued their exploration of the trail system's natural vistas. Shelli was euphoric about the numerous scenic picture ops to add to her photo journal.

On one of the trails they came across a plaque with the inscription, "Lewis and Clark in Illinois—In the fall of 1803 Captain Meriwether Lewis and William Clark passed this place with about twenty men on their way westward. At the confluence of the Wabash and Ohio Rivers, they first reached territory that is now the state of Illinois. Then they turned their boats south on the Ohio toward Fort Massac."

James commented, "This area is full of history. I may actually be able to use this trip in some of my research and classes."

Shelli sighed, "Remember, no shop talk on this trip!"

"Let's move on," Pat urged, "It's beginning to get dark. We need to get back to the vehicle while we can still see. We would not want to get lost out here."

As darkness began to envelope the couples, James noticed a sign bearing the words which he read aloud, "Slaves used these natural hills and hollows for shelter and hiding places from slave bounty hunters. The slaves would usually cross the Ohio River during periods of time when the river was low. They escaped from slave-holding states to the 'freedom' state of Illinois."

After a moment of silence, he resumed, "Can you imagine slaves moving through this area at night fleeing from bounty hunters and their tracking dogs. Think about the terror going through their minds as they ran for their lives. Thoughts of being beaten, captured, and returned to cruel masters, or being sold to even worse masters plagued their every step. All they were trying to do was experience freedom and equality!"

When the exhausted hikers returned to their vehicle, the sun had almost vanished behind the dark outline of the Southern Illinois hills. The journey back to the inn was quiet. As he drove, visions of desperate slaves and their pursuers haunted James' thoughts and reminded him of the old journal he had read the night before.

Suddenly, Shelli's alarmed voice sounded from the back seat, "Watch out, James, there's a deer about to cross the road!" As Shelli's warning was heard, the deer ran into the path of the Navigator. James braked frantically! All was well. As the deer disappeared into the darkness, James and Shelli regained their composure for the second time on the trip. The first was a near miss collision with a Chicago cab, and now it was a deer on a country road.

"Boy, that was a close call!" Robert said nervously.

"I'll say!" agreed James.

The tired couples continued their short trip back to the old inn. As they drove up the winding drive, they met a car coming down the hill. They also noticed an extra car in the parking area.

"The other guests must have arrived while we were exploring," Pat observed.

"Yes, it looks that way. Who did Nick and Carla say they were expecting?" Shelli asked.

"I don't recall them saying who the other guests are," James answered. "I guess we'll find out soon."

James took a parking space next to the other car. He noticed it had an out-of-state license plate.

"Whoever they are, they had a long drive!" Robert noted. "Their tag says 'South Dakota'."

The couples unloaded the day's gear and ascended the steps to the inn. While standing on the front porch, the couples heard voices and sounds of laughter escaping through the old front door. Smells of dinner permeated the chilly night air.

James set down the lunch basket and turned the doorknob. The door was locked. He rang the doorbell, and the laughter stopped abruptly. A voice from inside the house called out. "Coming, hang on!"

Nick opened the door to allow the hikers to enter the front hall. He said, "Sorry, the door must have locked accidentally." He took Carla's lunch basket from James. Nick continued, "Great timing, we were just about to go into the dining room for dinner. Oh, and we want you to meet our new guests."

Robert replied, "That sounds good to me; I'm starved!" Pat grabbed her husband by the sleeve and prodded him toward the staircase.

"Give us a few minutes to put away our gear, freshen up, and we'll be right down," Shelli responded to Nick's invitation.

Upstairs the couples quickly changed into informal attire. The house seemed much quieter than the night before for some reason. The rooms had been tidied with fresh linens, soaps, and candles. Carla had thoughtfully placed mints on the freshly made beds. The duos met at the top of the stairs and descended quickly. Nick and Carla were putting the finishing touches on the dinner meal, and the new couple was already seated at the dining table.

Nick made the introduction of the new guests, "I would like you to meet Ed and Paige Waters. They are all the way from South Dakota!"

"Pleased to meet you. We noticed your license plate when we drove up. You are a long way from home," James spoke for his party. "I'm James Carlton and this is my wife, Shelli, and our friends, Robert and Pat Cain. We are from the Chicago area."

Ed responded to James' friendly introduction, "Nick was telling Paige and me about their Chicago guests. We've been to the 'Windy City' a couple of times to shop and see the sights. We're not used to that much traffic and hustle and bustle! Like they say, 'a nice place to visit, but I wouldn't want to live there'," Ed said with a frown.

Paige joked, "Oh, don't pay any attention to him; he gets nervous any time he has to drive in heavy traffic."

After introductions and small talk, the old inn's patrons and owners enjoyed another one of Carla's fine meals. The conversation was lively. The new guests were enthusiastic and elated to be on their trip to Hickory Hill.

"By the way, Nick, was that another guest we met coming down the driveway?" James questioned.

Nick glanced quickly toward Ed and answered, "Oh, no, that was just someone asking for directions."

The exhausted Chicago natives retired to their rooms for the night. James and Shelli recounted the adventures of the day when James was reminded of one of the signs they had seen on the trail. "Remember the slave sign we read today?" James asked.

"Sure, I do. What about it, James?" quizzed Shelli.

"It made me start thinking about the hidden journal I told all of you about this morning," James said wearily.

"What about that journal, hon?" grilled Shelli. "I want to see your great 'find' of the trip."

James motioned his wife over to his overnight bag. The two of them peered eagerly into the darkness of the box's hiding place, and James reached in carefully and exposed the old box. The journal had been placed back into its resting place in the early hours of the morning. It was soon to be purged of more of its secrets.

"Oh, James, this is a 'find'! I know you will enjoy its historical pages. But, you're going to have to read them without me. I'm exhausted again tonight!" Shelli's voice echoed softly in her husband's ear. "Sweet dreams, I love you. I'm going to take a nice, hot bath and get a good night's sleep for our trip back tomorrow."

James kissed his wife good night and opened the pages of the old journal. The lamp's soft light gave the pages an eerie glow; he found his early morning stopping place. He once again traveled back in time via the slightly faded ink and yellowed pages of the journal. He began to read in a soft, muffled voice.

June 10, 1871

My business started makin money. I needed more workers. I didnt want to rent any more slaves from over in Livingston County than I had last year. I mentioned this to one of the men I had doin some overseein work for me. He said that there was lots of slaves that had made their way acrost the river when the water was down. Why didnt we just catch some

of those runaways and workem. He started me
thinkin so I told him to round up some of his men
that I could trust and we would jest take care of
some of those runaways ourselves. Slaves cost money.
It made sense to me to not only work em in the salt
works but make another business out of em while I
was keepin em up. Ole Clyde and his cousin Russell
did a lot of work for me that winter. Clyde noed a
man named Harmon. Harmon and his brother
Hardin was patrollers acrost the river in Kaintucky
They owned some good trackin dogs that had a good
nose for them runaways. The brothers were supposed
to keep the slaves in line at night and check on the
slaves to keep down an uprisin. They were supposed
to punish the uppity niggers but sometimes they jest
helped em disappear. I gave em a ten dollar gold
piece every time they found and brought me one of
those slaves from over acrost the river. They thought
they was makin a lot of money. It was enough to buy
their whiskey and tobacky. I used the bucks to work
in the salt and I had another job for the bitches. I
wanted to make sure I got each nights cargo myself.
When I built this house for my beloved wife Sina I
had three stories built. We only used two floors for
the family. Me and my wife had ten younguns. Not
all of em lived to be growed up. My hand grows
weary now.

July 4, 1871

Independence day dont mean much to me anymore.
At one time things round here was a lot different
than they are today. On July 4 years ago I had the
boys workin upstairs gitten ready for another delivry
that night. I caint remember all the details but these
I do remember. While the family was getting ready
for a big celebration with a big dinner and music I
had some of my boys buildin holdin stalls for the new
bitches. I had to keep em upstairs so nobody would
no they was here. My men had already finished the
carriage doors so we could bring those niggers in the
wagon right on in to the house at night. I had em to
fix a stairs that went to the attic. But I remember
that July 4 like it was yesterday. The boys finished
the attic jest like I told em to. I had several small
rooms built up there to hold delivrys. I told em to
put some iron rings up there so we could bolt down
some shackles if need be. I told em I wanted a post
in the middle of the attic so those niggers could
watch the whipins so they wouldn't be thinkin bout
runin away or talkin back. Uncle Bob he was my prize
stud nigger. He would do anything for all the steak
eggs biscuits and sawmill gravy he could hold. Yeah
he was a dandy he was. I used him for the bitches. I
raised me up some niggers that could do that

backbreakin work I had to do when I was a youngun. Not any more though I am the master now. A bitch that is going to have a youngun brung more money if I was to sell er.

July 11, 1871

I feel poorly. My leg hurts me somethin awful tonight. I dont have that leg anymore but it still hurts. I wont never forgit that day I lost it. I was whopin Abigail cause she dropped a washin of my white shirts. She was my pick of the bitches. I gave uncle Bob his orders that I had better never catch him with her iffen he noed what was good for him. I had to show her who was master on this hill. I could not let her git away with that. All them other slaves would of thought they could of dun the same thing. One of them young nigger bucks came up behind me with a ax. He threw me down on the ground before I noed what was happenin. One of em held me down and the other one hacked off my leg with that ax. I thought I was gonna die before my men could get that leg tied off. I layed up in the bed for weeks. I had the fever bad and went out of my head. The ole doc tole me I almost met my maker but I showed em who was master of this hill again. They never tried anythang like that no more no sir. I tole my *overseer to ship Abigail south. I think she was going to have a baby. Miss Sina never noed it.*

It was getting late when James laid aside the old journal. He couldn't believe some of the awful things he had just read. He turned out the reading lamp and started to bed when he heard voices. Who else was still up this time of night? He thought he heard the sound of a baby crying. Could the old house be projecting strange sounds or maybe it was the wind of the fall night. He strained his hearing trying to detect if he had really heard something. A small, faint cry permeated the stillness. He had heard something!

He walked quietly to their bedroom door. There was a dim light slithering through the crack at the bottom of it. Should he open the door or not? He decided to listen more closely. He heard some people talking quietly as they descended the old staircase. Then he heard what he thought was the front door to the inn open and close softly. James, intrigued, walked over to the east window of the room. He peered into the darkness of the night and noticed the interior light go on in the Dakota couple's car. James heard the motor start, and he watched the car drive slowly out of the parking lot. The headlights remained off until the vehicle was halfway down the driveway. That was strange he thought to himself. Why would they be leaving at this time of night? This mystery couldn't be solved tonight James thought to himself. The weekend getaway was almost over. The trip back to Chicago tomorrow would be tiring. He had to get some sleep tonight because the journal had stolen it for two nights.

It was early Sunday morning when James finally got his much needed rest--but not for long. Shelli was up early packing and getting belongings ready for the trip back home. James was sleeping so soundly that she hated to awaken her prince, but it was time to leave the peaceful countryside for the pavement, construction, and traffic of the "Windy City".

They would have a quick continental breakfast to start the new day and their drive north. The fall getaway was over. They had enjoyed their short time away from work and the hectic pace of the big city.

The couples met downstairs after quick showers and last minute checks of their rooms. They wanted to leave nothing behind and take only memories. Shelli and Pat had decided the night before that they would enjoy coming back to this part of the state in the spring. There was still exploring to do. The wildflowers, dogwood and red bud trees would look beautiful that time of year. The night before they all agreed to come back to Hickory Hill, and the women made the arrangements with Carla for a week in the springtime. They wanted the same rooms and hospitality they had received on this trip!

After short good-byes and thanks to the innkeepers, James and Robert loaded the Navigator. James noticed the Dakota couple's car was still gone. For an instant his memory flashed back to last night's observation from his window. Shelli and Pat brought coffee and some of Carla's freshly baked blueberry muffins to share with the guys. The cups of coffee steamed in the early fall Southern Illinois morning. Shelli took a deep breath of fresh air and made a sigh before she entered the SUV. It was going to be a lovely day.

The weekenders drove the winding driveway of the inn as the sun was peeking over the trees in the distance. Their branches reached out as though they were beckoning the couples' return. Shelli wanted to take one last photo of their journey. She asked Robert, who had switched from navigator to driver on the return trip, to stop at the end of the driveway. Shelli opened the door and stepped into the nippy fall air. Her camera focused on the imposing old house sitting on the hill. The camera's shutter clicked. While the film rewound in Shelli's camera, James' thoughts turned to the visions that had been captured on the film, the old wooden box, and the journal's words that had enslaved his interest.

Robert turned out of the driveway and immediately met a yellow cab driving slowly toward the entrance of the inn. He glanced in his side mirror and noticed the cab entering Hickory Hill's driveway. "That's strange," Robert commented.

"What's strange?" Pat asked.

"That yellow cab out here in the middle of nowhere, and it turned in the B & B's driveway," Robert answered his wife's question.

"That is strange, and it looked like a teenage girl was the only passenger in the cab," noticed Pat.

James jumped into the conversation with some of his observations, "Several strange things have been going on around here. Remember the car we met in the drive last night? Nick gave a quick explanation of who it was, and this morning before daylight I heard voices in the hall and the other couple's car left. This morning their car was still gone."

"What voices in the hall?" inquired Shelli.

James sighed impatiently, "Oh, it was just something that happened before I went to bed last night. We'll discuss it later."

Forty-five minutes after leaving the inn the couples were back on the interstate. The husbands swapped out driving on the return trip while their wives reminisced about experiences of the last several days. Discussion of work and everyday life crept into the conversation occasionally. However, James was preoccupied. He was pondering something. He felt he had been transported to another place and time.

The mile markers clicked off much faster than they did on the trip down. But, "you always get back quicker than you came," James thought to himself.

Chapter 4 The Mission

The Christmas lights and decorations on Michigan Avenue were truly "magnificent" this time of year. The red and green garlands and lights outlining the avenue contrasted against the white, stinging snow being blown violently from Lake Michigan. The holiday season was being ushered in by one of the biggest snowstorms of the season.

The couples had been back in their work routine for several weeks since their fall trip. James had worked feverishly grading end-of-semester papers and posting grades for students before Christmas break. Robert had been busy with his clients at the stock exchange. Pat and Shelli had been involved with a new cell memory research project at the medical center. The couples had enjoyed some weekend dinner dates at Randalini's, their favorite restaurant in the city, and had attended a few holiday musicals. Other than those occasional social outings, they had not been together much since the fall break weekend.

December furiously showed its strength outside as James sat quietly resting in his favorite chair. His thoughts turned from students and grades to the worn journal he had purchased on their Southern Illinois trip. Shelli was still at work when he began searching the house for the yellowed pages that had intrigued him during their stay on their fall retreat. James searched his desk thoroughly and then checked closets and bookshelves to no avail. He decided to build a fire and settle down in his easy chair and await the arrival of the "keeper" of the house, Shelli.

The couple's schedule in the last few months had hindered the professor's progress in reading any other entries in the Crenshaw journal. James drifted off to sleep still thinking about the historic words. A dream returned him to the last entry he had read. The description of the whipping post in the recorded lines became real. His mind took him back to the 1800's in the attic of Crenshaw's house. His dream was so real that he could feel the whip cutting into his flesh. The next crack of the whip made James flinch so hard that it woke him with a guttural moan. The loud whimper frightened Shelli as she entered the room, and she dropped the bundle of Christmas packages she was carrying. "You scared me! What's wrong, James?"

"I had the weirdest dream. I thought I was back in Crenshaw's old house, and he was whipping me at the post in his attic," James, still visibly shaken, answered weakly. "By the way, Shelli, where is the journal I bought on our trip? I've looked everywhere. What did you do with it?"

"What did *I* do with it?" she replied, annoyed, after a long day at work. "Do you know the road conditions on Lakeshore Drive? I just barely made it through the snow and Christmas shoppers. It's wild out there! Give me a few minutes to collect my thoughts and rest. It has to be here somewhere." Shelli settled down into her favorite chair and clicked on the news. She reached under the table next to her chair for the *TV Guide* and unearthed the misplaced journal. "It's right here where you put it when we returned from our trip. Sometimes you have to remove the clutter to find things of value."

"Now who's being the philosophical one?" James replied with a grin on his face. He liked it when he could reverse one of Shelli's favorite remarks.

Shelli ceremoniously handed over the focus of her husband's search. "I'm going to set the table and warm the carry-out. Don't get too involved; we'll be ready to eat shortly."

James settled back in his chair with his rediscovered treasure. The aromas from the kitchen mixed with visions of a new entry of John Hart Crenshaw.

July 29, 1871

As I set here on this hot July night I can smell the honeysuckle in the heavy night air. I hear the faint sound of a whippoorwill over in my field. The corn is makin good this year. We have had some good rains. This land has been good to me and my family first with the salt works and timber and now farmin. Pa wouldnt have noed what to do with this much land if he had had it but I showed them all. The slave money might of stoped but the land goes on makin money. Yes land is the only thing that lasts but you have to take care of it. I took care of the land and it took care of Miss Sina our younguns and me.

After dinner James read more entries from Crenshaw's diary which rekindled his interest in the words penned on the old pages.

August 8, 1871

I thought about old Kuykendall today. I was thinking back to '42 how the law tried to put us in jail for takin those niggers comin acrost the river. That trial was short. They couldnt prove nothing on us. They couldnt find a white man to testify in that court room. If they knowed what was good for them they would keep their mouths shut. My eyes and hand grow weary.

August 11, 1871

The salt works just could not make me money any more after those fokes started those salt works in Virginny and Ohio. Most of my land had already been cleared of the timber when I started farmin many years ago. Every stump was pulled up. Those niggers worked up this rich ground and planted my crops. I had them to work from sunup to sundown. My overseer made sure they worked or they would *feel the sting of his whip. Yes ifin I hadnt started that salt business years ago I still would be some old sharecropper farmin somebody elses land and not a penny to show for what I did. Yessir all this land is mine now.*

James' reaction to the entries was even more appalling than he had remembered. Peering over his reading glasses at his wife in the chair next to him, he said with repulsion, "Shelli, these entries of Crenshaw are so horrendous in the way he treated his slaves I feel compelled to research this man, where he lived, his business transactions, and any public documentation of what this man did.

She answered encouragingly, "Why don't you start with the internet?"

"That's a good idea. Where's the laptop?" James inquired.

He eagerly typed "John Hart Crenshaw" into Northwestern's Research Library website. To his disappointment, no results were found. After Northwestern, he tried the SIU (Southern Illinois University) website. "Your search for 'John Hart Crenshaw' returned no results" came up again. Next, he tried several search engines to no avail. "This is proving harder than I thought," James commented. "I'm finding no entries on the internet. I may have to do more personal research on this one. I know he is from Southern Illinois from the entries I have read so far."

"When are we going back down state? I may have to track down some primary sources on this man. He is eluding any evidence of his existence."

"We have plans to return to that area for our 'spring fling'," Shelli reminded him.

James was pacified with the prospect of better research results when they revisited the southern end of the state. "I think I will start with the local court house records and also see if I can track down any resource people. I might even visit SIU to see if I can find any information not on their website."

"That sounds like a plan to me. You and Robert can research while Pat and I shop, see the sights, and snap some photos. I'm tired. Remember I'VE got to get up early in the morning. Some of us are still working. I hope the snow plows have done their job."

"OK, I'm going to read a couple more entries before I go to bed," sighed James.

Shelli replied cautiously, "Remember how engrossed you became with that journal at the B & B and the dreams it spawned."

"I know, but I have to do it. It's become a mission for me to solve the mystery of this evil man who bought, sold, re-captured, tortured, and even bred human beings as if they were animals. I'm a history professor, yet before I found this journal, I was totally unaware that this particular person existed. I've read about the atrocities of slavery in history books, but this is the first time I've read in a person's own handwriting about what he did and how he thought. It puts a face on it!"

James decided to lay aside the old journal during the Christmas holidays. He wanted his wife's vacation time to be pleasant and free of his preoccupation with Crenshaw. Shelli's Christmas baking included preparing a brunch for Robert and Pat. While she was serving the meal, Pat reminisced, "Robert, this reminds me of the great brunch we had at Hickory Hill in the fall."

Robert agreed, "You're right, Pat! Hey, Shelli, do you have any maple syrup for this French toast? I'm glad we are going back to that place. Carla is such a great cook. I love her idea of comfort foods."

The word "comfort" triggered James' thoughts of the "discomfort" he had felt while reading the entries in Crenshaw's journal. He had promised himself he was not going to think about the journal or talk about it during the Christmas holidays.

Shelli, replying to Robert's comment said, "I'm glad my cooking reminds you of some of the great meals we enjoyed during our retreat. By the way, we still haven't explored Cave-in-Rock. I need some photos to complete my scrapbook project that I started when we returned from our fall getaway."

Pat encouraged her, "You won't have long to wait. The months are slipping away. It will be time for our spring trip soon."

*   *   *

Weeks passed quickly and Valentine's Day weekend found the foursome at Randalini's, their favorite restaurant in the city. The two couples enjoyed a romantic candlelight meal. After a dessert of "Murder by Chocolate" mousse cake and Kona coffee, conversation gravitated to one of their favorite subjects—vacation days.

Work at the research clinic had been stressful with long hours and tedious preparations for an upcoming conference in the city. The women desperately needed a break. The men were just as eager to take days off from work. James was having a difficult time keeping his mind on his classes. He was preoccupied with the upcoming research of John Hart Crenshaw he planned to do during their spring visit to Southern Illinois. Life for Robert and Pat was equally busy. Robert was stressed by the grueling demands of a challenging farm futures market.

As James and Shelli were driving back to Evanston, they discussed his research of Crenshaw. He recalled the unproductive search he had done via the internet. Thinking of that, he reminded Shelli, "Don't forget the work I want to do when we go to Gallatin County next month. I know you want us all to visit Cave-in-Rock, but after that outing, Robert agreed to help me with my research. Hopefully, people in the community, perhaps local historians, have some information on John Hart Crenshaw. Maybe they can direct me to other primary sources. From his entries, I know he lived somewhere around the small town of Equality. You and Pat can shop, sightsee, take pictures, or whatever you would like to do."

"That sounds like a plan to me. Pat and I can do some exploring on our own. I'm sure she would like to check out some of the local vintage clothing shops," agreed Shelli.

During the last several miles of the drive home, James' thoughts cued in on the last few pages he had read in Crenshaw's journal. The entries had almost relinquished their presentments of evil. Ghostly hauntings played havoc with James' mind as he observed the eerie fog rolling in from Lake Michigan nearly obscuring the entrance to their driveway. "I'm glad we are home safely; the weather is so foreboding tonight," sighed Shelli. James, not expecting her comment, shot a piercing glance in her direction. It was as if his mate had read his thoughts.

Once in the house, Shelli informed James of her intentions, "I'm going to take a shower and go to bed. I'm exhausted. That drive home was draining."

"OK, I'll join you shortly. I want to read the next entry in the old journal before I go to bed."

James slumped into his favorite chair beside the luminous glow of the antique lamp. He began reading. . .

October 16, 1871

Tonight my memories take me back to the time Mr. Abraham Lincoln visited my home. He was ridin the circuit at that time and was very interested in politicking. I remember we rode horses over my land and I showed him where the land had brung me. Me

and him grew up about alike. He told me he grew up
por and that his Pa had been kind of like mine. He
could be mean at times and expected hard work for
nothin. Mr Lincoln wanted to do great things. He
got book learnin on his own but I wanted to get rich.
When he saw my niggers workin I could tell by his
words and looks that he didnt like what he seen. No
nevermind to me. I noed how them politicans were.
Some of them think they are better than you but
they dont think things they do are bad. I was
important in the south part of the state and he noed
it. He told me how he used to see slaves being took
down the road by his Pas place in Kaintucky. He said
slavery was an injustice. It was money to me. He
had this kind of fancy talk about how he got
educated himself and made a lawyer. I grew up por
just like he did. Now I have land and a good business.
What did he have? Some dream about being
somebody important. Well he got his dream all right.
But what did it bring him? A war and then
somebody shot him because he thought them niggers
should vote. Yep Mr. Lincoln its been about six years
ago now that you got yourself kilt.

November 27, 1871

My bones are cold tonight. The fall winds seem to be
findin their way through every crack in the house.
My breathin aint been good these last few weeks. Ole
doc was out here today. He told me to stay out of
this cold damp weather. He said I was gonna git the
comsumtion ifin I dont do what he says. Miss Sina is
gittin ready for a big dinner. She and all her house
slaves are runnin around doin all kinds of cleanin and
fixin food. We used to have some big gathrins in this
house. I remember the play parties and music. I
cant do much anymore. I had to git Sam to help me
run things round here. I can trust him to do me
right ifin he does things I aint liken he nos what
happens. My sleep last night was restless. I heared
voices in my sleep like they was talkin aw it was jest
somethin I et for supper that unsettled my ole belly.
My ole body gits tired fast now. I gotta go to bed.

December 3, 1871

My hand is shaken so bad I dont no ifin I can writ.
My breathin is harder jest like the old doc said it
would git. Dont no how much longer this bad feelin
will last. Miss Sina had one of her house slaves brang
me up some supper. I aint hungry it jest dont seem
right bein in this house all the time now. I need to be

out there showin Sam what needs to be done. I thought I saw one of my boys last night I musta bin dreamin cause I no he died a long time ago. Jest like four of my other younguns did. I got this feelin I aint gonna be here much longer. I took care of my family. Thats more than I can say for my Pa. I got my land and money thats all any man needs in this life. I did good. I did right by these people round here. I gave money to the church in town. What else is there anyway? Tomorr I think I will. . .

Chapter 5 The Cave Adventure

The time passed quickly between Valentine's Day and spring break. James needed time away from books and schedules. Pat and Robert yearned for time away from doctors' appointments, fertility tests, and discussions of adoption. Shelli was always ready to sharpen her photography skills. The couples were packed and ready to leave for their spring trip south when the day finally arrived.

The couples drove straight through to their destination at Hickory Hill. Anxious not to waste time, there were no side trip adventures on this outing. The women were as eager to utilize as many days sightseeing and shopping as the men were researching the annals of the old journal belonging to John Hart Crenshaw. Since the men and the women were going to be spending time on different quests, the couples drove their own vehicles. The adventurous duos were going to be sure to include a trip to Cave-in-Rock State Park. This jaunt had not fit into their rushed schedule on their first trip down to Southern Illinois.

The travel weary pairs were greeted at Hickory Hill by the familiar faces of Nick and Carla. As requested, the same rooms were available from their previous trip.

The Chicago guests checked in and later enjoyed some of Carla's famous country cuisine. That was something they, especially Robert, had been looking forward to for months.

After a restful night in the old house, James was up early planning his strategy for the research he was about to begin. He was happy that Robert was willing to be recruited to help in his endeavor to delve into the life and misdeeds of John Hart Crenshaw. For the first leg of their research project, they were going to the SIU Library, then on to the Gallatin County Courthouse. But today was set aside for their delayed excursion to Cave-in-Rock. After dressing and enjoying a big country breakfast, the foursome boarded the Navigator to embark on their adventure.

As the couples left the B & B for their outing to Cave-in-Rock, they noticed the radiant yellow blooms of the jonquils and the pregnant buds of the dogwood trees peering back at them. Shelli observed the landscape and commented, "Isn't spring a promising season. Notice the barren terrain in contrast to the new signs of life— Stop!—I have to take a picture." Soon the sign "Welcome to Cave-in-Rock State Park" appeared.

The modern day explorers were excited as their vehicle easily climbed the hill overlooking the Ohio River. What a view! The scenic overlook spread a spectacular sight before their eyes. They wondered how it must have looked when the Native Americans lived in this area many years ago. James, the group's historian, had ingrained into them the historical significance of every scene until it was second nature.

Robert said excitedly, "I think this exploration is going to be fun," as he pulled another worn brochure from his back pocket. Robert directed the other explorers to the panoramic overlook of the Ohio River. "Oh, good," Robert observed, "the river is down so we should be able to go into the cave. I read some interesting facts about the area in this brochure I picked up at the Visitor's Center on our last trip. It said the cave was used by local Native Americans. Archaeologists found some cave drawings that dated back to early tribes in this region. The cave was also used by river pirates to wait for settlers who were traveling down the Ohio to get to the Mississippi River on the way to New Orleans. The pirates would use all kinds of ploys to get the people on the flatboats to come ashore or pick them up. The pirates robbed and sometimes killed everyone on board and took their boats. Supposedly, counterfeiters who worked in this area would pass off their bad money to settlers going down the river."

Robert continued, "I also read that a man named Wilson turned the cave into a dwelling and liquor joint. I bet that attracted a lot of river people! The information stated that he worked with some other deceitful people.

Then, they took advantage of those poor folks minding their own business trying to go south. From what I read, old Wilson even had women, or should I say 'ladies of the evening', working for him. He would get the men drunk then turn them over to the women for a little nightly entertainment. Often they were robbed. The next morning the men who had been passing through woke up with a splitting headache if they woke up at all."

"It sounds like Cave-in-Rock was a lively place," James interjected.

"Do you remember that movie made back in the 1960's called *How the West Was Won*? Well, Jimmy Stewart played a man that got mixed up with some of those river pirates. That part of the film was shot here in Cave-in-Rock," Robert added.

"I remember Jimmy Stewart playing that part. I used to show that movie when I taught U.S. history to high school students. I can't wait to see this place," replied James.

Shelli was especially interested in the beautiful vista from the camera's eye. She loved to take landscape pictures. There was a great photo op at every turn. The old friends decided to walk some of the trails in the park before they explored the cave. All of the city dwellers wanted to observe the flora and fauna of the area. They were in luck. They spotted a whitetail deer in the distance. He was sniffing the air to alert himself of any nearby danger as he grazed leisurely on the succulent grass. The squirrels scampered quickly in front of the group as they trudged up and down the hills. Songbirds entertained with a variety of notes. The dogwood trees were not in bloom here either, but their swollen buds would soon show their beautiful white cross-shaped flowers. Shelli constantly clicked the shutter on her camera. She set up her tripod several times for a foursome photo. She wanted to capture this adventure for years to come.

After hiking over some of the rough terrain in the park, Robert decided that it was time for the group to eat. "Let's try the lodge restaurant," suggested Pat.

"Sounds great to me," Shelli agreed.

The couples entered the quaint park café. It afforded the couples a beautiful view of the river and the lodge rental cabins below. The friendly waitress welcomed them to the park and handed them menus. After getting their drink orders she asked, "Where do you folks live? What is your interest in this area?"

"Helen," James answered as he read her name tag. "We are staying at a bed and breakfast close to Equality called Hickory Hill."

"I'm not familiar with that inn," Helen replied. It must be a new establishment."

Shelli chimed in on the conversation, "Yes, it is a new business in an old structure! We found its advertisement on the internet. You know these rental cabins would be a great place to stay if we come back to this area later."

"They would," agreed Pat.

While they were waiting for their food, James and Robert looked at the many pictures displayed on the walls of the small eatery. Robert spotted a picture taken in the 60's of Jimmy Stewart playing the part of a buckskin-clad character in the movie *How the West Was Won.* Robert was elated as he invited the other three to share in his discovery. "See, I told you about that movie! Remember, part of it was filmed right here. I can hardly wait to scout the cave."

The girls browsed the gift shop. Shelli was most interested in the postcard section. She couldn't pass up a great photo no matter who imprisoned the vision. Robert and James were already seated when their wives returned from the gift shop. The women had small sacks of goodies. They couldn't pass up a unique souvenir.

"I'm starved," said Robert.

"I am too," agreed James.

The waitress brought the scrumptious smelling entrees they had selected. The famished couples devoured almost every morsel on their plates. "Would you care for dessert?" questioned the gracious server.

"Why not?" Robert spoke for the group.

"Our chocolate pecan pie is the best anywhere around!" she bragged.

"Great!" exclaimed Robert, "Bring us four of your largest pieces. We still have a lot of hiking to do, and we may need the extra energy."

"Would you like to make that a la mode?" quizzed the waitress.

"Why not," Shelli reasoned, "Pat and I normally share a dessert, but we're forgetting about dieting while we're on vacation."

The couples enjoyed their pie and coffee as they observed several large barges going downstream. James said in his professor voice, "I wonder if they are going all the way to New Orleans? Can't you imagine what adventures this very hill we are sitting on has seen in years past?"

Robert responded, "Yes, and I wonder what kind of cargo the barges are carrying?"

The local ferry had made several trips across the river while the vacationers were exploring the park. From the hill, the vehicles on the ferry boat had looked like Match Box cars.

"It was interesting to watch how carefully the ferry's pilot had to coordinate the speed of the boat with the river current and oncoming barges. We're used to seeing large vessels on Lake Michigan, but this was a new experience for us," Robert continued.

James suggested, "Let's take the ferry, so we can say we also visited Kentucky on this trip." It was approved. They would cross the river.

Robert asked, "Is everyone finished eating? It's getting late. We need to explore the cave while we still have plenty of light." Everyone agreed. While the men took care of the checks and tip, the women moved quickly to the door to avoid the temptation of visiting the gift shop again.

Everybody loaded into the Navigator and set off for the highlight of the day—the cave in the rock. The steps leading down to the cave area were only a short distance from the restaurant. When the vehicle came to a stop, the women were first out of the SUV. They were ready for this quest. Shelli realized she needed to insert a new memory card into her digital camera. She shouted to the other three, "Hey, wait for me!" Shelli was proud of her new camera. It had been one of her Christmas presents from James. She had been using her old 35mm camera when they were down in the fall.

They stopped first at the natural opening in the top of the cave. It had a barrier built up around it to help keep onlookers safe. The group standing on tiptoes peered down into the hole. The dark abyss ensnared each one's curiosity as to what lay beneath his feet. The switchback concrete steps were steep as they descended to the cave area. "This is beautiful!" gasped Shelli as she began snapping pictures.

"Yes, I'm glad the river is down, so we can go inside," Robert said with a thrill in his voice.

As the couples entered the mouth of the cave, Robert cautioned, " Watch your footing. The floor has several raised areas that are worn and slick from so many footsteps in the past. It isn't a deep cave. It doesn't intrude into the hill a long distance, but it is fairly wide and has a high ceiling."

As sunlight filtered down from the opening in the roof, Shelli exclaimed, "Look, there's the hole in the top we were looking down into when we first got here."

"It looks different from down here," added Pat.

James walked over to the cave's wall and ran his hand over the rough texture of the rock, "I know there is so much history contained in these walls. Can you imagine the campfires of the Native Americans, the torch lights of the river pirates, and the voices that permeated the night air? I can even imagine this being a shelter of some kind for slaves that had crossed the river. Think of the hardships those people endured trying to attain their freedom," James reflected.

Everyone was absorbed in his or her own mental vision. Their imaginations conjured up the many things that could have happened in this very area where they

now stood and walked. The damp feeling of the cave's
air and the echoes of their voices against the cave's walls
emitted an eerie sensation as the four explorers continued
their excursion.

What dark secrets had been kept in these walls over
the years? This was the question that plagued James as
he continued his examination of the cavern. He couldn't
help but be reminded of some of the journal entries
Crenshaw penned in the 1800's about what could have
been this very place.

Back outside, Shelli gathered everyone in front of the
cave entrance for a group photo. She set up her tripod
and attached her camera. "OK, everyone ready?" she
asked.

"Ready as we will ever be," answered Pat.

Shelli set the timer on her camera and quickly slipped
into the group as everyone said, "You make me smile."
The camera's shutter clicked and clicked again. Another

historical moment in time for the old cave had been captured.

The tourists loaded once again into the SUV and headed for the ferry crossing ramp. They had only a short wait for the boat to reach their side of the river. The pilot hit his mark, and the ferry was in place. The deckhand wrapped the chains and directed the cars and trucks to exit. He then motioned for James to drive up on the deck of the ferry. As the Navigator made its way onto the vessel, the creaking and popping sounds of metal against metal made the women a little hesitant of this venture. After some reassuring from Robert, Shelli and Pat settled back to enjoy the ride.

Shelli let her window down, pressed the video button on the camera, and began narrating the excursion. The ferry crossed the Ohio successfully, and the cars rolled onto the Kentucky shore. The explorers decided to make the short drive to Marion, Kentucky, before returning to the river. On the trip back, they passed several Amish buggies on the road. This was a reminder of their fall trip and the night they had spent in Arthur.

The sun was slipping past a dark cloud bank as the vacationers pulled into the drive leading up to Hickory Hill. It had been another day filled with adventure. The beds at the old inn offered a restful night to the weary guests and prepared them for another day's adventure.

After a delectable breakfast consisting of omelets, home fries, and homemade breakfast pastries, the men began their mission. The women decided to relax a little longer over another cup of coffee. While Carla was clearing the table, the girls' conversation turned to their plans for the day which included finding some vintage clothing shops. "Carla," asked Pat, "we plan to shop today. We would like to find some 40's era clothing. Do you know of any shops in the area?"

"Yes, there are several antique stores in Equality that may have something you're looking for, and there is a vintage boutique on the main street," Carla informed her patrons. She bustled out with dirty dishes and returned through the swinging doors that connected the kitchen to the dining room. On her way to clear the buffet still laden with food, she overheard the conversation turn to Pat and Robert's failed attempts to conceive.

"This is so relaxing," Pat sipped her aromatic dark roast coffee and sighed, "I have been so tired of tests and the constant plague on my emotions of futile attempts to conceive. My biological clock is ticking, and the resolution is eluding me. Robert and I have had numerous tests with no scientific "raison d'être" for us not being able to have a baby."

Shelli, trying to lighten the mood, responded "Well, Parle vu France', Madame. When did you start speaking French?" The girls shared a good-hearted laugh and resumed their conversation about shopping. Carla, having heard this chat, tuned in more closely as she attempted to find other chores in the dining room.

Shelli interjected, "Changing the subject, I want to take some snapshots of us together. I have a few more photos on my memory card; then we can get the pictures developed while we are out shopping today."

Shelli noticed their hostess was still in the dining room and asked, "Carla, where is the nearest store I can get my digital pictures printed?"

Carla responded, "Harrisburg would be the closest big town. Its Walmart has a photo center. Then, it's only about ten miles from Harrisburg to Equality to the vintage clothing store you asked about. Harrisburg may have some shops. It's larger than Equality; ask while you are there about vintage clothing."

Shelli quickly changed the subject, "Let me get my tripod out of the SUV, and I'll take some pictures of us in front of the inn. I haven't taken very many photos of the two of us on this trip."

"Let's freshen up first, and then we'll meet on the porch," suggested Pat always concerned about her appearance. They disappeared upstairs for a few minutes and then met on the front steps.

When the friends opened the door of the inn, the bright spring sun met them eagerly. "Oh, great," exclaimed Shelli excitedly, "the morning sun is the perfect lighting for our pictures. Let me set up the tripod and camera, and we'll be in business."

Pat made herself comfortable on the front porch steps while her friend busied herself setting her tripod and camera at just the right spot. "Do you want me to move? Where are you going to stage this 'photo shoot'?" questioned Pat, always the fashion plate.

"Oh, Pat, you are always photogenic!" Shelli answered with a sigh. "Let me get everything in focus, and we'll be ready." Shelli pushed the timer button on the camera and quickly ran over and sat down next to her best friend. The duo posed as the camera shutter clicked twice.

Shelli instructed Pat to move up a couple of steps, "Let me take a few more pictures from a different angle." She picked up the camera and tripod and planted it farther from the house. After leveling the legs on the tripod, the amateur photographer looked through the viewfinder and burst out joyfully, "This will be a great picture! I can see all three stories of the house in the background." Her artist's eye was pleased with the aesthetics of the picture.

Once again Shelli pushed the timer button and scurried to join her friend for the last couple of photos left on the memory card. "That's a 'wrap' as they say in the movies. Let's get these printed. I can't wait to see the photos I've taken so far on this trip."

"It's only ten o'clock. We have plenty of time to go to Harrisburg to get your pictures printed and rummage through some vintage clothing stores," Pat quickly agreed.

The two friends climbed into their vehicle and headed toward Harrisburg to start the day's venture. "Maybe you will find some ideas about maternity clothes in some of the shops," encouraged Shelli. The girls chatted as the miles slipped by quickly from Hickory Hill to Harrisburg, Illinois. The Harrisburg city limits came into view. . .

Chapter 6 A Link to the Past

The former college roommates discussed some of the interesting points of yesterday's exploration when they spotted the local Walmart. "Great, we're here. I need to pick up a few personal items," said Pat.

"While you do that, I can print our pictures," replied Shelli. "Meet me at the photo center when you finish. I'm sure it will take me a while. I will probably have to crop and do some other 'technical enhancements' before I print."

"OK," answered Pat, "see you in a while." Pat grabbed a shopping cart while Shelli started looking for the photo center.

"Ah, there it is," she thought as she spotted the direction sign near the ceiling of the store. She headed straight for the sign. Like most photographers, she was anxious to see what masterpieces would emerge from her memory card.

Pat gave the cosmetic counter the "once-over" for some of the things she needed; she was always on the lookout for bargains. She tried a new fragrance. "That was a maybe," she thought. Pat decided on several items and moved on to another department in the store.

Shelli arrived at the photo center quickly after spotting its sign. She found a processing machine that was not in use and quickly popped the memory card into the proper slot. The processor immediately began to display its instructions. Shelli was familiar with this particular brand of printer, so she went to work. After going through the initial steps, all of the pictures that had been stored on the SD card gazed back at her from the monitor as she quickly touched the screen to fast forward the photos.

She began her quest of cropping, zooming in and out, and eliminating photos to print. In the back of her mind, she remembered an old photography class she had once taken. Two statements always stood out in her memory when she was printing pictures. The first, "You are very fortunate if you get several 'good' photos from a roll."

And the second was, "A picture is worth a thousand words". So far, Shelli had been pleased with the pictures she had taken on this trip.

Pat made her way toward the Electronics Department when she spotted the baby section of the store. She stopped and looked longingly at the latest infant apparel and baby care products. They stirred that feeling inside her once more. She lost track of time, but she knew Shelli well enough by now to know that she was in her own little world while being creative with the printing machine. Pat hoped her friend Shelli would create a photographic journal of her new baby someday.

Pat was right. Shelli chose her photos carefully. She was elated to find more borders and different graphics on this machine than she had used on other printers. She was in "printer's heaven". She was now touching the monitor screen with lightning speed accuracy! She couldn't help but compare this new technology with the old "put your film in a mailing envelope and see what you get back" method of developing pictures. Yes, photography had come a long way since she had been interested in capturing memories.

Pat finally eased her way out of the baby department into ladies' clothing. She was definitely a shopper when it came to clothes—new or vintage. Shelli continued her work at the printer as she mumbled to herself, "Boy, I didn't realize how many photos we took yesterday not counting the ones I took this morning." Shelli didn't mind; it wasn't work for her—it was "art". After looking at all the photos, eliminating duplicates and "not-so-good" shots, she proceeded to put borders on some, crop others, and insert text on some of the photos before she prepared to print. As Shelli touched the screen to start the printing process, Pat appeared in the aisle next to her.

Shelli commented to her friend, "Finished shopping already?"

"Already?" Pat replied, "We have been here over two hours!"

"Are you sure?" questioned Shelli.

"Yes, I checked my watch when I got the cart."

"Well, you know what they say 'Time flies when you're having fun'. I'm ready to print. You can stay and help me collect the photos. I made duplicates of each one, and they will be coming out on both sides of the machine. We don't want to forget any of them. I can't wait for you and 'the boys' to see some of the masterpieces we created."

The photo printer began its developing process. The 4" X 6" prints emerged from the machine as if to say "Here we come—wait until you see us!" Pat and Shelli were patient as each photo was ejected from the processor. They were like two children waiting for gumballs to drop from a machine. With each photo, the excitement swelled! Finally, all the prints had been delivered. The task was complete.

Shelli gave the prints to the friendly clerk behind the counter. He quickly counted the photos, put them in an envelope stamped with a bar code, and handed them back to her. "I hope you enjoy these, ma'am," the clerk said politely.

"Thanks, I'm sure we will," replied Shelli. Then, she took the envelope of imprinted memories and placed them in Pat's shopping cart. "I have a few things to pick up, and I will be ready to check out," she informed her fellow shopper.

"OK, I'm finished. I'll follow you," said Pat.

Shelli's shopping didn't take long, and the two made their way to a check-out counter. Pat emptied the cart onto the counter's conveyor belt. The cashier made conversation with the vacationers as she scanned each item. Pat quizzed the cashier about vintage clothing stores in town. She was anxious to continue her shopping spree.

The clerk was very helpful in giving directions to the nearby Visitor's Center. "They should have brochures for shopping, restaurants, and other attractions," she informed the customers. Pat and Shelli each paid for her own purchases and shared the cost of the photos. One of today's tasks had been completed.

As the duo made their way to the SUV in the parking lot, they looked at each other and said, "I'm hungry." They laughed because the two knew each other so well it wasn't a surprise they thought so much alike.

"How about a burger and fries?" Pat suggested.

"I'm famished; a juicy burger would be great," Shelli replied. "It's such a nice day; let's pick up our burgers at a drive-through and eat in the SUV. When we finish, we can look at our pictures."

"Sounds good to me," Pat agreed. After finding their favorite fast-food restaurant and picking up their orders, they parked and enjoyed the beautiful weather, food, and fellowship. Lunches devoured, the viewing of the pictures could wait no longer. The girls were eager to inspect the photographs Shelli had so meticulously printed. Shelli opened the envelope the clerk in the store had given her. She began looking at each photo carefully in one set of the pictures. Then she handed each one to Pat. They were in awe of the images before their eyes. Friends enjoying each other's company, beautiful vistas, historical sites, and nature's wonders had been captured.

The last photos viewed by the two were the ones taken of themselves that morning before leaving. Shelli looked at the first two of the morning's pictures. She was pleased when she described the effective lighting in the photographs. After studying the photographs with an observant photographer's eye, she quickly handed them to Pat and went on to the last three pictures taken of them sitting on the front steps.

Shelli insisted, "Let me see those pics again." Holding two of the pictures of the girls on the steps, she asked, "Pat, can you see any difference in these photos?"

Pat replied, "You know I'm no shutterbug. They both look the same to me except I'm waving in the last one."

"Look at the window on the top floor of the house," instructed Shelli. "Notice the old shutters inside the window are closed in the first, but they are partly opened in the other photo. I can barely see a shadowy outline of someone in the window in the last picture."

Pat agreed, "Yes, I can see now that I look more closely. That's strange. Didn't Nick tell us when we first came to Hickory Hill they still had not renovated the third floor?"

"You are right, Pat," Shelli nodded in agreement. Carla was downstairs when we went out the front door, and Nick was out using the field mower when we left. I wonder who could have been watching our photo shoot?"

The women decided to leave the mystery unsolved for now as they pulled out of the parking lot. The eager shoppers had plans to scour Harrisburg for vintage clothing and other dress shops. While Shelli was an artist at heart, Pat was a shopper. Any shop intrigued her. Using the directions they had gotten from the cashier at Walmart, they found the local Visitor's Center. From the counter there, they picked up lists of shops, restaurants, and local tourist attractions. Shelli would have been content to shoot pictures of the local gardens and architecture, but Pat insisted that today was a shopping day. "Don't even look at the local 'hot spots'," teased Pat, "you promised that today we would shop."

"I know. We are, but if there is time left in our day, there are some interesting sights in this town," returned

Shelli good-naturedly. She knew there would be no time left with Pat along.

The antique shops were very interesting, but vintage clothing was not their specialty. Pat found some estate jewelry she liked and bought several old brooches and crystal beads. She also purchased a couple of old hats which had probably been Easter bonnets in their day. "What are you going to do with those brooches?" questioned Shelli.

"I'll wear some of them and use some in decorating," Pat was quick to reply. "I will use a couple on my jackets and frame the others as art," she added.

*   *   *

While the girls were shopping, the men were already on their mission to research John Hart Crenshaw. On the way to SIU (Southern Illinois University) in Carbondale,

James updated Robert on the latest entries of the old journal. Robert, usually all business, was stunned at the inhumane words from the past. "No wonder your mind has been someplace else for the last few months. I suspected something was bothering you, but I didn't know what. I knew you were reading the journal, but I figured it was boring farm records," said Robert. "I'll be glad to help you research. I'm not as good at it as you are, but I'll do what I can," he added.

The men headed into the library after they found a visitor's parking space. Accustomed to historical research, James knew his way around the library stacks. The researchers spent several hours to no avail looking for records on John Hart Crenshaw. They browsed through reference books, other hard copies, and sat at a computer looking for information. James was frustrated that so little information was available in the library or on the internet. Librarians were able to locate information on the Saline River and the salt works but nothing on Crenshaw. Reluctantly, the friends left to try their luck at the Gallatin County Courthouse.

"I don't understand why we're not finding information on this man," commented James on the way to Shawneetown.

"Maybe the journal is fiction. Did you ever think of that? Maybe this guy was a writer, and he fantasized rather than actually doing those horrible things," suggested Robert.

"I don't think so. It's a journal written as an autobiography. It's an account of his life, his boyhood, his rise to riches, his total disregard for human life, and his feelings about his life. I think it's real, but why don't we know about him? He sounds like an atrocious villain like others in history, but his story is untold. I want to know more about him and expose him to the world if he is as bad as I think," shuddered James as he spoke. "You know, some of those slaves could have been relatives of mine or Shelli's," James admitted verbally for the first time.

"What good would that do? He died years ago. His deeds can not be undone even if it's true," countered Robert.

"I know, but the people he tortured, bred, and sold need their stories told," returned James barely above a whisper.

When the men arrived at the court house in Shawneetown, they approached the first clerk they saw in the deed records office. "Hello, my name is Bill. How can I help you today?"

"I'd like to find some records on John Hart Crenshaw who lived in Gallatin County in the 1800's," James requested.

"I'm sorry; the court house flooded in 1937. Many of our 1800's records were lost. You are welcome to search what we do have," informed the clerk.

The men searched the few documents available, but found little useful information on this man. Taking the record books, James returned to the counter. Bill, the friendly clerk, smiled and asked, "What kind of information do you want on this Crenshaw man?"

"I want records of his holdings, court records-- anything I can find. I discovered a journal written by him, and I want to track down any kind of information I can. I've been to the SIU library, but no material was available. I believe he was a slave owner and operated the salt works in this area for several years," added James.

"I don't know if this will mean anything to you, but there was an elderly black man living in Equality who told an oral history of a former slave owner. I'm not sure whether the stories were about this Crenshaw man. That name sounds familiar. I have no way of knowing if the stories are true, but they are intriguing," informed the clerk. "I heard some of the stories myself when I was a child growing up near Equality. His name was Mr. John Wilkes."

The men returned to the car, and James looked at the address and directions given to him by the court clerk. "I don't want to get my hopes up, but this could be what I'm looking for. A person living today could not have known Crenshaw personally, but maybe he has heard stories. Oral history is better than no history."

"There's only one way to find out. We'll unlock this mystery one way or another," remarked Robert getting caught up in James' enthusiasm for uncovering a long lost story.

After enjoying the short drive from Shawneetown to Equality, James pulled into the driveway of a modest

white frame house on a tree-lined street. The wooden
steps creaked as the two men stepped up. The screen
door protested louder as James opened it and knocked on
the front door. An elderly gentleman in a clean set of
khaki work clothes answered the door. He was thin and
slightly bent. His voice was strong and deep as he asked
the two strangers what they needed.

"Hello, Mr. Wilkes, I'm James Carlton. I live in
Evanston, and I'm here in Southern Illinois with my wife
and friends on a vacation. We are staying at a bed and
breakfast near here called Hickory Hill. On the way
down last fall, we stopped at Arthur, Illinois, for the
night and did some shopping. I found an old antique box
with a false bottom. Inside was a leather-bound
yellowed journal written by John Hart Crenshaw. It
contained some disturbing entries. I was given your
name at the court house as someone who tells an oral

history of a local slave owner. Could it be this man?" inquired James hopefully.

Tears welled up in the old man's eyes. His body shook slightly as if he had had a cold chill. "I have heared tell about that journal all my life," he softly replied with a quaver in his voice. "Stories have been handed down in my family for generations about the cruel master who beat, maimed, and bred slaves working for him. I had no evidence, so I could not prove the stories were true. I had always heard tell of ole Crenshaw's journal. Some of the young'uns would have to fetch it for him when he wanted to write."

"We'd be forever grateful if you would share those stories with us," pleaded James.

"I'll be glad to tell you what I know," replied the old gentleman softly. The storyteller invited his guests to have a seat on his neat front porch. Then he began speaking with a trembling voice. "Crenshaw was an evil man. He had no morals, no human compassion at all. He bred slaves in his own home. He sold the babies and pregnant women. He hunted down free slaves and sold 'em or forced 'em back into slavery at the salt works or his farm. It was a business to him. He worked them til they dropped; he beat and tortured those who stood up to him or who tried to escape. He captured free slaves and forced 'em to work, and he bred 'em like cattle. Now, mind you, these stories are jest things I have heared all my life. My great-grandfather and one of his cousins saw Crenshaw whippin' a female slave and his cousin tried to stop him with an ax. He hacked off one of Crenshaw's legs. He was meaner than ever after he got better."

"What happened to your great-grandfather and his cousin?" asked James.

"We don't know; no one ever saw his cousin again."

"No one ever saw his cousin again?" James looked puzzled.

"No, the story was that the ole master beat him and sold him or had him killed. Of course, we don't know for sure," replied the old man through tear-filled eyes.

"Why was the woman being beaten by Crenshaw?" questioned Robert.

"She accidentally dropped a tub of Crenshaw's white shirts on the ground."

"And your great-grandfather and his cousin tried to stop him?" inquired James.

"Yes, ole poppa was a gentleman; he couldn't allow a woman to be beaten without trying to help. They had been splittin' wood nearby so his cousin had an ax in his hand. He was able to swing it a few times at Crenshaw's legs before some of the overseers knocked him down."

"What happened to the woman? Do you know?" Robert jumped into the conversation.

"Yes, and what happened to your great-grandfather?" interjected James.

"The woman disappeared, too, jest like the cousin." A lump came in his throat at this point. All three men sat in silence a moment before any of them could speak. "My great-grandfather was whipped and carried the scars the rest of his life."

"Do you think the man or the woman could have escaped?" Robert was finally able to ask.

"It's possible, I reckon, but not likely. There were a few neighbors here at the time who disapproved of Crenshaw's cruelty, but they were afraid of him too. Besides, he used blood hounds; he usually caught whatever he was after."

"I'd like to know more about this man. Will you help me?" James implored.

"I don't know what I can do other than share with you the handed-down stories. I'll do that." A faint smile appeared on the elderly man's face as James extended his hand. The handshake turned into an embrace. The two shared a reverence for the history of their people. Tears streamed down Robert's face also. "I have an Abraham Lincoln story. Would you like to hear it?" offered the old man.

"Yes, I would very much like to hear it," said James eagerly.

"My grandfather was just a boy when it happened; he was bout fourteen years old, and he remembered every word of it. He was helping his mother set up a big, long table outside to feed Abe Lincoln and some of them other people that was politicin'. He heard the whole conversation between Crenshaw and Mr. Lincoln." All three men slipped back into the past and relived the scene through a slave boy's eyes. As the old man told the story, James envisioned this event as if viewing a documentary on the History Channel. The story began...

*   *   *

"Mr. Lincoln," an invited guest, a neighbor of John Hart Crenshaw's, slipped quietly up to Mr. Lincoln and said, "If John walks up, I'm going to change the subject."

"That sounds ominous," replied Mr. Lincoln.

"If that means evil, then yes, it is. It is evil what goes on here. Keep your eyes and ears open; ask questions. The worst kind of slavery goes on here. I can't say much; I'm afraid for my family. I do what I can, but it's not enough."

"What's not enough?" questioned Crenshaw who had walked up quietly behind the neighbor.

"Rain—we need a lot more if the crops are to be plentiful," returned the startled but composed neighbor.

"Rain? We've had a fair amount, but I guess we could use some more. We've had worse years," remarked Crenshaw. "Would you like a tour of Hickory Hill, Mr. Lincoln?

"Hickory Hill?" James interrupted the old man's story. "Do you mean, Mr. Wilkes, that the old inn where we are staying was Crenshaw's house?"

"Oh, yes, I thought, you boys, knowed that."

"I'm sorry I interrupted your story, Mr. John, but I'm shocked that we are staying in the very house you are describing!"

"Oh, yes, its kept that name all these years. Where was I?" Mr. John continued the story. . .

Crenshaw boasted, "I'm very proud of my estate— Hickory Hill. It took me many years to get where I am so I don't mind showin' off a bit. I started at the salt works, and now I own all the farm land you see."

"I am always ready to oblige a citizen's desire to brag a little, Mr. Crenshaw. Hard work and ambition have their rewards," stated Mr. Lincoln.

As the story continued, James envisioned Crenshaw leading the lanky Lincoln around the grounds. The old man's grandfather as a boy was taken along to hold the horses when the men dismounted.

Crenshaw stopped beside a whipping post. "This is the secret of my success. You have to teach slaves who's boss. Work 'em til they drop. They're replaced easily enough. They're not worth their salt if they get too soft," chuckled Crenshaw at his own joke.

"You're talking about human beings—not animals, Mr. Crenshaw," responded a startled Lincoln.

"Have you ever owned slaves, Mr. Lincoln?" quizzed the offended host.

"No, I have not and will not."

"Then, I don't think you can speak with authority on the subject, do you?" retorted John. "I own thousands of acres; I couldn't operate without them," he added defensively.

"As I am a member of the human race myself, I believe I can speak with authority. Beating and working to death another human being is profoundly wrong. People are born with certain unalienable rights. One is to be free of bondage," Mr. Lincoln spoke with a deep, full voice which quavered slightly with emotion as he spoke.

"See here, you have no idea what it takes to run a salt work or a farm. I have to use them niggers; I couldn't run them salt works or farm this land without them. I worked hard when I was just a boy. I worked my way up. I deserve to be the boss. I used brute strength and brains to get where I am today," continued Crenshaw.

"But you were compensated, and you were a free man. That's the difference."

"These niggers don't know how to own and operate a business. Their brute strength is all they have."

"They're men, Mr. Crenshaw, God-created men."

"They're inferior men meant to be owned and ruled by superior men," resounded Crenshaw.

*　　　*　　　*

Physically and emotionally drained, Robert looked down at his watch. He noticed how quickly time had passed as they listened to the old man's stories. "James, it's getting late. Our wives will be worried about us," Robert coaxed.

"You're right, Robert," James agreed as he turned back to the storyteller. "Mr. John, would you mind if we come back tomorrow to hear more. Maybe other stories will come to mind after a little rest."

"I'd be pleased if you would come back."

The men said good-bye and looked forward to their next meeting. Later, the couples met back at the inn after a productive day for all. Both the men and the women had new mysteries to be solved. After dinner, the couples retired to James and Shelli's room to look at the pictures and discuss the day's events. The girls shared their day talking about their adventure of shopping and picture printing in Harrisburg. They had spent so much time in Harrisburg they didn't have time to check out the shops in Equality.

The friends looked at the trip's pictures when Shelli remembered the last photos she had taken that morning. She shuffled through the stack of prints and looked carefully for the two she and Pat had compared earlier in the day. "Ah, here they are," she exclaimed. "James, I want you and Robert to take a look at these pictures. They were taken this morning before we left for Harrisburg. I used my tripod and set the camera's timer."

He scrutinized the photographs with the aid of the bright reading lamp on the table. "What am I supposed to be looking for?" quizzed James.

"Hold the photos side by side and tell me if you see anything unusual about them," Shelli instructed.

James looked closer and called Robert over to get his opinion. "I still don't see any difference," James said.

"Can't you see it?" Shelli questioned fretfully. "Look at the window on the top floor. In the first photo the shutter is closed. In the second one, the shutter is partly open, and you can see what looks like someone peering from the window. Didn't Nick and Carla tell us at dinner last night that they still had not renovated all the top floor? Carla was downstairs when this picture was taken, and Nick was out on the mower, and there were no other vehicles in the parking lot when we left. Pat and I can't figure out who could have been watching us this morning."

James said with a skeptical laugh, "It must be the lighting or some fluke on the print."

"Maybe," said Shelli, "but I think there was someone up there. I don't know who-- yet."

The couples finished looking at the photos then turned to the men's explorations. "Well," James said with a little mystery in his own voice, "you won't believe what these two detectives discovered today!" James pointed to Robert and himself proudly.

"We checked out SIU with no luck. Dead end. Just like the internet. Then we returned to Equality. By the way, I thought we would spot you girls in town, but I can see now how 'busy' you were," James said with a little sarcasm in his voice.

Shelli gave her husband a friendly "love tap" on his shoulder and told him to continue his story. "First, we went to the county court house in Shawneetown hoping to find some records about John Hart Crenshaw. We were told that the courthouse had been flooded many years ago, and most of the old records were lost. I was really disappointed and started to walk out the door when the man assisting us asked me what I was looking for.

He said he might be able to help in some way. I told him I was looking for any records pertaining to John H. Crenshaw. He remembered many years ago when he was a boy, he had heard a story from an old black gentleman about a man who could have been Crenshaw. My ears perked up with that comment. I asked if the old man were still living. He didn't know for sure, but he assisted us with the census records, death records, and property records. According to all of the records, we concluded he was still alive. The clerk gave us the man's last known address and directions to the house. Off we went on our quest. Bingo! We hit pay-dirt, ladies. You can't even begin to know what Mr. Wilkes told us." Finally, James shared a portion of the information they had obtained from the local oral historian.

It was late into the night when the couples finished talking about the day's discoveries. Robert and Pat went to their room, and James and Shelli readied themselves for bed. It had been a long day, but neither of them could get what were now yesterday's events out of their minds. They lay in bed in a loving embrace quietly discussing the stories the old man had told. Shelli questioned her husband, "Do you think the old gentleman really knows what he is talking about, or if his tales could have been made up in an aging mind with progressing dementia?"

James insisted, "Shelli, that man told us things that I read myself in Crenshaw's journal. That convinced me what he told us HAD TO BE the truth. The journal entries confirmed his story to me. I didn't mention this in front of Pat, but Mr. Wilkes said this very house we are in right now belonged to John Hart Crenshaw himself."

Shelli gasped, "Are you sure?"

"Yes," James replied. "He had gotten this information handed down to him through past generations. Most people in this area are deceased now that would have known anything about the previous owners, and most of the records were lost in the flood."

"Wow!" exclaimed Shelli, "That is astonishing!"

"We thought about not telling you girls right now, because we wanted to do a little more investigating tomorrow."

"I wonder if Nick and Carla know about the story?" inquired Shelli.

"I don't know, but somehow Robert and I are going to find out. The old man said this house is still known for its strange 'goings on'."

"What do you suppose he meant by that?"

"I don't know, but the more I think about what he said, and now with the pictures you showed us tonight, the more I am determined to research this house and its history!"

Later in the night, James was awakened by voices and car doors closing in the parking lot. He quietly slipped out of bed being careful not to awaken Shelli. Cautiously, he walked to the window and peered out into the darkness. He observed with the aid of the interior lights of the vehicle what appeared to be a young girl stepping out. Nick seemed to be assisting her. Why was she here in the middle of the night James wondered? His thoughts quickly took him back to their fall trip when they had seen another young girl arriving by taxi. The words of the elderly gentleman they spoke to echoed in his head about the strange things that still happen in the slave breeder's house.

James observed secretly so the people outside would not know they were being watched. Nick walked the girl up to the large front porch. James heard a slight creaking of the front door and then low voices. All was quiet once again. His ears strained to hear any more sounds, but a strange quietness permeated the night. He slipped quietly back into bed, but sleep escaped him.

Later, James' thoughts were still on his early morning's observation when Shelli awoke. He shared with her what he had seen and heard. "What time was it?" she inquired. "I didn't hear anything."

"I think it was about 5:30 because it wasn't long until daylight."

His wife replied, "Did you get any sleep at all when you came back to bed?"

"No, my mind was trying to fit the parts of this dark puzzle together. More pieces are beginning to come into the light!"

Chapter 7 Mystery of the Third Floor

James made sure Nick and Carla were not in earshot. Then, he shared the previous night's events with Robert and Pat while the couples had their morning coffee and homemade pastries. Shelli and Pat opted to forget the shopping quest and join their husbands to solve the new found mystery. The picture with the shadow in the upstairs window stirred their curiosity even more now. The girls decided to assist by using *their* research skills. After breakfast they enthusiastically set off for the public library in Equality. While there, they would make inquiries about old newspaper articles and local church records.

In response to his invitation, James and Robert returned to the home of the elderly gentleman. They had hopes of gleaning more information from the depths of the old man's memory.

As they drove down the driveway leading to the small, neat, white frame house, both of the men were in deep thought and anticipation as to what new clues of their mystery might be unraveled. Mr. John was standing inside the screen door as if waiting for the opportunity to reveal memories that had been conjured up since yesterday's conversation.

The old storyteller's feet shuffled along the freshly swept porch as he opened the screen door for his visitors. He turned to them and asked, "Would, you boys, like to have some fresh brewed coffee?"

Robert replied, "I'd love some," while James nodded in agreement. The coffee smelled inviting in the spring morning air. They couldn't resist the fragrant aroma and the old man's hospitality.

"Come on in this house, then, and have a seat." After Mr. John served the two young men, they both noticed the unusual way he served himself. He slowly poured

147

some of the contents of the cup into the saucer and then proceeded to blow on it. He then drank from his saucer. Neither of the men had ever seen this method of drinking coffee before. James, with his inquisitive mind asked, "Mr. John, that's an unusual way to drink coffee. Where did you learn to drink it like that?"

The old man smiled as he shared the coffee story with the young men. "I've been drinkin' coffee as long as I can remember. I used to see my pappy and uncles drink theirs this way. They always said it helped cool it off. You know in the old days we used to boil our coffee. We didn't have these new-fangled coffee makers like we have today. Why, these things today tell you almost everything. I guess I jest got in the habit of drinkin' it this way, and that's the only way I like it now." All three of the men had a good laugh.

"Well, that's OK, Mr. John," James reassured him. "I have never seen anyone drink coffee like that before."

"You jest ain't old enough," Mr. John answered with a smile as he shook his head slightly and slapped his knee.

"How old are you, Mr. John?" Robert questioned.

"I turned ninety-five last month! Now, boys, do you want to hear some more of them stories about Crenshaw? Well, I reckon I'll tell you some more about the big black man Crenshaw kept as his 'stud'." Mr. John started his new story with misty eyes and a slight tremble in his voice. The two men looked at each other and listened intently as the old gentlemen started to tell his tale.

"They called him 'Uncle Bob'," he started. "Crenshaw kept a big healthy stud slave he called Uncle Bob to breed a strong, healthy line of workers."

James interrupted, "I remember reading something in Crenshaw's journal about that man! Do you know his

149

last name?" James thumbed through the old, yellowed pages of the journal he had brought with him on this visit. "Yes, here it is. He wrote about 'Uncle Bob' in the July 4, 1871 entry. I knew I wanted to find out all I could about him."

The elderly historian leaned slightly forward and gently touched the leather binding of the old journal. As James kindly slipped the weathered book into Mr. John's equally weathered hands, the recipient moaned softly. "Oh, I can't believe it has happened. I am holding 'ole master's' journal. That is one of the stories I heared all my life. Some of my kin told me that their grandpappy when he was a boy would have to fetch ole Crenshaw's writin' book specially after he got his'n leg cut off."

"Yes, you told us about that yesterday," James kindly reminded him.

"I never really knowed iffen it was true, but now I know." He opened it slowly and carefully turned its brittle pages. The tears that had been merely welling up in his eyes now began to stream down his wrinkled cheeks. Slowly, he became aware of the present once again, and he blurted out "Wilson! That was his name."

Startled by the abrupt break in silence, James asked, "What did you say, Mr. John?"

"His last name was Wilson. I'm almost sure that was his name," replied the old man.

"I apologize for my interruption," James said politely. "Go on with your story."

Mr. John carefully held the leather-bound journal as he continued, "Well, I recollect them tellin' me that Crenshaw had 'Uncle Bob' to do his 'stud work'. He didn't make him work in the fields or do any hard labor. He was a 'house nigger'. He did chores around the house, and he did what Crenshaw wanted him to do— make babies. He was a real big man from what I heared my daddy and other men tell. They said they had been told 'Uncle Bob' was way over six feet tall. Some of them called him a 'Mandingo' or somethin' liken to that name. Yessir, he just stayed around the house and ate good, and mounted whatever black women Crenshaw brought him. I also heared tell he had a special 'breedin' room' upstairs where he went to take care of his business for Crenshaw. One of my uncles told me he heared tell that 'Uncle Bob' joined the Army during the Civil War. Now you know, boys, this is jest tales I heared about when I was growin' up. I don't know iffen any of this is true."

James confirmed the old man's story by reading him the entry from Crenshaw's journal. "I think the stories you have heard are about right, Mr. John," James answered. "According to the journal entry I just read to you, Crenshaw himself said how he used that man."

Mr. Wilkes continued telling his visitors the stories he had locked in his memory. They had stirred remembrances long forgotten.

"Well, Mr. John, we surely do appreciate your sharing your childhood recollections with us. We have some other errands to do in town. Would you mind if we come again tomorrow for a short visit? I would like to hear more about 'Uncle Bob'. Maybe you can remember something that might help us research him. We'll bring back the old journal, so you can inspect it more," James promised.

Mr. John shook his head and laughed, "You boys have been good for this old man. I ain't had such a good time visitin' in I don't know how long. After my dear wife died several years ago, I jest ain't had much interest in much of nothin'. I would be glad for you to come back."

*　　　*　　　*

While the men visited Mr. Wilkes, Shelli and Pat arrived at the small community library in Equality with a determination to aid in James' unraveling this new mystery. They checked periodicals, old newspaper clippings, local photos, and any other materials they thought might be helpful. All to no avail! This man they attempted to learn more about had lived over one hundred fifty years ago in this rural area in Illinois. They wondered what information *they* could dig up?

After several searches, a new hope surfaced. Their last search had been checking the internet connections for articles of some Southern Illinois newspapers. James had checked internet sites, but he had overlooked area papers. They hit pay dirt! One article they found was from the *Illinois Republican* newspaper in Shawneetown, Illinois. The article told of Crenshaw's alleged activity in slave kidnappings and his indictment on two different counts. He was never convicted due to the fact that the kidnapping of slaves was so difficult to prove. The slaves had to be taken out of state in order to be considered kidnapped. That was almost impossible for any prosecutor in that day to prove. How was the movement of the slaves to be traced?

The girls continued to check other newspapers in the southern part of the state. Additional articles were also found concerning Crenshaw. One article dated in the 1830's stated that it was believed that Crenshaw's "night runs" involved the use of wagons to haul his captives to one of several residences belonging to him at the time. The article also said that it was believed that he even went as far as to have large doors built into his house. The driver of the wagon could pull into the house and the doors could be closed behind him and his "cargo" unloaded! Another article alluded to kidnapped Negroes being kept under the eaves of the house in something like an attic or hidden rooms.

When the sleuths read this article, they looked at each other as a "light bulb" turned on in their brains simultaneously! Shelli spoke first, "Remember the first grand tour we took of Hickory Hill back in the fall?"

Pat interrupted, "Are you thinking the same thing I am thinking, Shelli? Remember the place on the outside of the house where it looked like doors had been at one time, and the space was filled in? This proves the bed and breakfast *is* the same Hickory Hill that the old man told our husbands about."

"Yes," answered Shelli, "that's exactly what I was thinking. And what about the article that mentioned the attic? The third floor," she added. "Remember Nick told us part of it had been sealed off," she recalled. "Now, more than ever, I know someone was in that attic when we took our pictures yesterday morning! This mystery has just begun."

"This story is getting spookier by the minute; I can't wait to tell the guys about our new findings," Pat shuddered. The women made copies of the articles purged from the internet. They were eager to get back to the inn to share what *they* had discovered and see if their husbands had gotten any more information from Mr. Wilkes.

As the friends traveled back on the rural road, they drove up behind a slow-moving Amish wagon. Their conversation quickly went back to a day much like this one when a free Negro might have been stopped by some of Crenshaw's men and taken back to the very place where they would now have to spend the night.

A truck with Kansas plates was in the parking lot when Pat and Shelli drove up. They assumed new guests had arrived and thought nothing unusual about it. Unfortunately, their husbands had failed to return from their quest. Both glanced up at the third floor window as they stepped out of the vehicle. This morning it was just an ordinary window, but now it was a window to the past. A car was heard as they reached the front steps of the porch. The wives were delighted their husbands had returned. The men hurriedly met them on the front porch. After a quick peck on the cheek for each wife, the men began telling their stories. Shelli and Pat jumped in and insisted their story be told first. They had so much to tell.

The four of them found a comfortable seat at a large round table on the huge front porch. Both the girls and the guys were excited to share today's discoveries. The women were absolutely bubbling; they couldn't wait to show their husbands what good investigative reporters they had been. The men told their wives to share their findings first. During the animated discussion, each person was mesmerized by the unearthing of the dark details from the past. The four amateur detectives each took a turn in relating what had been uncovered in the day's work. Realizing how each story authenticated the other, the couples sat in amazement at how today's events had ended. The most important discovery so far was that the B & B, Hickory Hill, **had** once belonged to John Hart Crenshaw!

Unknown to the friends, Carla had been dusting the inside window sill while their conversation had been taking place. She had stood perfectly still and listened at the partially opened window. She realized the creaking floor of the old house would alert her guests to the interest she showed in their discussion. Carla was taken aback but not surprised by what she had overheard. She knew from their dialogue these guests were interested in her old house and its past. What if they became suspicious of the secrets it is now hiding?

The couples continued sharing their day's discoveries as the spring sun began its descent behind the trees in the field next to the house. The late afternoon air was sweetly perfumed with the fragrance of early blooming honeysuckle intertwined with the smell of freshly mowed grass. Shelli, with a slight shiver in her voice, suggested they all go inside and ready themselves for a country dinner.

Carla had finished dusting and had almost finished the evening meal when she heard the couples open the front door. She quickly left the kitchen stove and greeted her guests as if they had just returned. "Supper will be ready shortly if you want to freshen up," Carla suggested.

"Whatever you are cooking smells heavenly," Shelli complimented their hostess.

"We'll be right down," interjected Robert who was always ready to eat.

The country comfort food was superb as all of their meals had been at Hickory Hill. Nick introduced the inn's newest guests, Lee and Shea Miller, before everyone began enjoying their evening meal. Pat reacted to Nick's introduction by addressing the couple, "This is our second trip down from Chicago, and we love the place. It's great to get out of the city. We love the food and the country setting," Pat praised their hosts and accommodations. "We noticed your beautiful truck as we came into the parking lot. Your license plate is from Kansas. What brings you to this country inn?"

Before the husband of the new couple could answer Pat, Nick quickly changed the subject to the weather forecast. "It is supposed to rain, and we could possibly have some stormy weather. I hope I can get my mowing finished before the rain comes. We can have some intense storms this time of year. The threat of tornadoes is possible according to the weather forecast I heard on tonight's news," Nick informed the group.

The dinner conversation changed gears to several other subjects before dessert. "Carla, you have outdone yourself once again!" Shelli congratulated the "chef". "This carrot cake is wonderful. How about giving up your secret?"

Carla, busying herself clearing the dirty dishes, quickly turned and with a somewhat startled look at Shelli said, "Excuse me?"

"The cake, Carla, would you be willing to give up your recipe?" Shelli clarified the question.

"Oh, the cake, certainly; I'll be glad to share it with you," Carla answered sheepishly.

After dinner, the four couples visited and shared background information. Nick told the group a little about himself, and he also bragged that Carla had been a pediatric nurse several years ago. Pat was interested in Carla's former occupation and began a conversation with her while the others continued to enjoy chatting about current events and the economy.

The time slipped by quickly. James glanced at his watch, "Wow, it's getting late." He looked at Shelli and asked, "Don't you think it is time to get some sleep? We have had a full day." Shelli nodded. Robert and Pat agreed. The friends excused themselves and went up the old stairs to their rooms. Another day had ended with excitement and more discoveries. James' mystery was slowly unraveling.

After the couples had retired for the night, lightning flashed in the western sky. It was streak lightning like giant fingers reaching from the clouds to the earth. Claps of thunder followed the strikes. The old house shook with each roll of thunder. Some of the original glass panes of the old windows rattled, and the rooms were filled with the fury of a Southern Illinois spring thunderstorm. The night lights flickered off and on several times during the height of the storm but recovered giving some sense of security to the guests.

The rain could be heard pelting the outside of the weathered house. The wind blew furiously, howling as it rounded the corners of the three-story dwelling. Then, the hail started to fall with tremendous force. It sounded like someone throwing "shooter" marbles on a metal roof. Was the old house the target of nature's wrath on this dark night?

After the storm moved eastward, the night air became settled. Now early spring tree frogs could be heard in the distance. It was an unusually warm night for this time of year even for Southern Illinois. The two upstate couples were not accustomed to storms of this magnitude this early in the spring.

The weather had everyone on edge. No one had a restful sleep. When the storm subsided, James dozed during the quietness of the night. His dreams of conversations with Mr. John continued to saturate his mind with haunting visions of past events that had happened at Hickory Hill.

Around three o'clock, another line of thunderstorms rolled across the countryside bringing with it more of nature's rage. The lightning and thunder were more intense in this storm than in the previous one. James was awakened from his dreams by a tremendous lightning strike to an old tree in a nearby fence row. Since the antique residence stood on a hill, it and all its surroundings were more susceptible to strikes. The lightning illuminated the entire room with an unusual glow. James could see the outline of all of the room and its contents. His mind was still groggy from his dreams.

He got out of bed and went to the east window in time to witness another strike of lightning close to the house. It shook the walls and the floor where he was standing. Shelli was in a deep sleep. She did not flinch as the ferocity of the storm seemed to be aimed at the aged structure and its occupants.

James decided to stay up and read over some of the notes he had taken from Mr. John's informative conversation. He sat down at the small reading table at the far corner of the room. The electricity was more stable since the second storm had moved east. He switched the reading lamp on to the lowest setting so he wouldn't disturb Shelli. James began going over his annotations. They brought back the feelings he had experienced while the old gentleman was sharing the stories he had suppressed for decades. He could not get the man called "Uncle Bob" out of his thoughts. Who was that man and what happened to him? What hold did Crenshaw have over him? What other kinds of hideous acts did Crenshaw make the man do? James read another entry about "Uncle Bob" in Crenshaw's journal.

Had he escaped or was he no longer needed for
Crenshaw's unspeakable demands?

James continued to explore his notes and remembered
Mr. John had told them Uncle Bob's last name. It was
Wilson. Mr. John had described Bob Wilson using
memories stored from his early childhood. He
remembered his uncles and grandfather relaying stories
they had heard in their lifetimes. According to Mr.
John's memory, Bob Wilson was a giant in stature. He
stood over six feet tall. He was very muscular; he was
not used as a field hand or for filling the huge vats with
salt water. He was used mainly as a "stud" to
impregnate Crenshaw's captured Negro women.
Crenshaw bred people like he would have bred cattle!
James' reflections ran rampant with the thought of that
unspeakable act. How could one human being subject
other human beings to such a despicable plan? It was all

about money! He did not care about the people he hurt. He thought only of getting richer.

In the early hours of the morning, James finished studying his notes and turned off the reading lamp. A quiet, steady rain was falling. Suddenly, he heard the sound of a car driving up to the parking area. He peered out the east window and saw a car with only its parking lights shining in the rain. It was a different vehicle than he had seen last night. It wasn't the Kansas couple's truck; it was still parked in the same place it had been when he and Robert returned to the inn yesterday afternoon.

James began to hear the faint sound of voices coming from the vehicle. He noticed someone getting out and saw a man who looked like Nick assisting the person. At that moment lightning danced from one cloud to another just enough to illuminate the predawn sky. James recognized the person lit by the electrified sky. The figures were more pronounced now--it was Nick.

James maintained his inconspicuous position behind the window draperies. Gazing through the glass, he observed Nick holding an umbrella for the stranger as they both stepped quickly toward the front porch. During another burst of lightning in the clouds, James saw what looked like a small satchel or bag being carried by the unidentified man. What was going on in the early morning hours at this old house? James' thoughts carried him again to what the aged black gentleman had said to him in their conversations. "There are strange 'goings on' at that house." Was he observing more of these "strange happenings" on this rainy morning? What was happening now at their "peaceful and serene" getaway to the past?

James continued watching the men. The creak of the old front door alerted him to the entrance of the pair into the downstairs hallway. He listened closely to hear any words or noises that would give him clues to the identification of the stranger. At that moment, James heard Nick speak Carla's name. Did Carla know the visitor? James quietly opened the door to his room hoping to hear more conversation between the men and Carla.

"Come on in out of this dreadful weather, doctor," James heard Carla's instruction. "You need to go up and check this one; we may have a problem," she continued. "You know where everything is, don't you?"

For the first time, James caught the sound of the voice from the stranger who had entered the house with Nick. "Yes, I do. Are you monitoring the blood pressure?" the stranger answered with a question.

At this point in the conversation the voices drifted out of James' hearing range. "Where have they gone? Why is a doctor making a house call in the middle of the night? It sounds like he has been here before. What's going on?" James said softly to himself.

As he quietly closed the bedroom door, Shelli began to stir from her deep sleep. She mumbled in a soft voice, "James, why are you out of bed? Is the storm over?" James reassured his wife with a gentle kiss to her forehead as he slipped back into bed. It would be daylight soon.

Chapter 8 "Uncle Bob"

The western sky was still dark with clouds pregnant with rain as James and Robert turned into Mr. John's driveway. They were like little boys again anticipating a good tale from an old storyteller. They could hardly wait to see if yesterday's conversation with their new found friend had summoned more memories of Crenshaw.

Mr. John slowly greeted his visitors at the front door. The old black man was humming "Amazing Grace". "I like that song you are humming, Mr. John," complimented James.

"Yes, that song was my wife's favorite hymn. For some reason, I love that old tune," he added.

"Do you know the history of that song, Mr. John?" the history professor asked.

"I don't reckon I do, young man."

"Well, that song was written by a man named John Newton. He was the captain of a slave ship. He would listen to the African chants of the slaves in the bowels of his ship at night. The story goes, the Lord convicted him about what he was doing on that ship, and he wrote the song. I've heard most Negro spirituals can be played using only the 'ebony keys' of a piano, and that song you were humming can be played using only those keys.

You don't even have to use the white ivory covered keys to play 'Amazing Grace'."

"That's an interesting story. I'm learning things I never knowed before," the old gentleman commented with a smile. "Looks like it's gonna rain again," Mr. John said with a somewhat trembling voice. "I sure hope it don't come another one of them bad storms. You know, you boys, got me to thinkin' last night about all those old stories again. Do you remember yesterday I told you about Uncle Bob? You asked me if I knowed what happened to him. I got to thinkin' about that, and I remembered something an uncle of mine told me many years ago. He said that he was told that Uncle Bob had joined the Army in the Civil War and had fought for the South. I don't know iffen he got killed or iffen he lived. Do you reckon there would be any record of him anywhere about that?" the old man directed his question to Robert.

"Yes," Robert answered, "if he were a soldier in the Confederate Army, there might be a record of his service. Right, James?"

"Yes," his friend affirmed, "that information will help us greatly in our research. I know there are some internet sites that deal with Civil War information. Mr. John, you've been a great help," James praised their new friend.

Mr. Wilkes shared several other memories he had recalled since their last visit. Their conversations had birthed more of his stories from the past. After hearing them, James and Robert were eager to go to the library and begin *their* search on the information they had garnered from Mr. John. They had much more information now to aid in their pursuit.

"I sure do appreciate, you young men, bringin' this old writin' book back today." Then, turning to James, he added profoundly, "These writins prove how our people were treated like animals and even bred like animals by some evil people like the person who wrote this here book." The two descendants of slaves looked at each other compassionately as the elder of the two slowly handed the journal back to James and quietly shook his head in disgust.

James and Robert said good bye to Mr. John Wilkes as they slowly made their way to the front porch. With each step, the men knew they were leaving the past and heading into the world of things not yet discovered. It was an exciting time for the two best buddies. Each bid his newly-found friend a good day. Both promised to visit the lonely old man again and share any new information.

As James turned his vehicle around and drove toward the street, he looked in his rear view mirror. Mr. John was still standing on the front steps of his modest home waving a good bye to the two men who had stirred up old memories.

The investigators quickly found Equality's modest public library. There was no problem navigating the small southern Illinois town. It seemed as if they were on a treasure hunt. The two could hardly wait to start digging. They could have used James' laptop with his wireless internet for the research, but both men working at once could do more research. There was a printer available at the library. Besides, James loved being in "the stacks" and rummaging through primary sources.

The guys entered the front door of the quaint, small town building housing the library. Glancing around quickly, they spotted the two computers their wives had used the day before. James, elated, commented, "Great! The two PC's are not being used. I'll take one, and you use the other one. We can do double the research."

"OK," Robert replied, "Got any suggestions as to where to start on this quest, history professor?"

James answered his fellow sleuth, "Yes, I can give you a couple of tips. First, search for 'Confederacy'. I have used that search before, but I don't recall much about it. Remember, Mr. John said that Uncle Bob fought for the South, so maybe you might find something. I'm going to try the *Journal of the Illinois State Historical Society.* It's also another website I'm familiar with in other projects I've done.

Both men immediately went to work after they brought up the internet. James began working on the Illinois Historical Society website and Robert on the Confederacy. They each tried several different websites that their searches produced until Robert clicked on "The Confederacy Project". There it was at the top of the third page he read---an entire article about Robert (Uncle Bob) Wilson. He quickly read the article and clicked on "print". Excited, he briefly shared part of the article's content with James before the printer could eject his treasured find. The men were ecstatic. "OK," Robert informed James. "I'm going to start here and search other references the article is giving me."

Meanwhile, James continued his search. He found several references in the I.H.S. website. He typed in "John Hart Crenshaw". "Guess what I have found?" James said in an electrified but subdued voice still respecting the library's "Quiet, Please" sign. "I have not only found an article that talks about Crenshaw but mentions Wilson's name as well."

The two men couldn't believe their eyes. Why hadn't James found these articles before? "Robert, we have hit the jackpot today!" The comrades acted as if they had won the lottery. After James printed his article, both men continued their mission for more cache the internet might be hiding in its millions and millions of bytes of information.

The library would soon close its doors for the day when the two amateur investigators printed out the last pages of new information. They paid the library attendant for the copies and thanked her for the assistance she had given them during the hours they had spent at the keyboards. Both were anxious to reread the printouts and decided not to wait until they got back to Hickory Hill. The guys had spotted a small cafe on their way to the library. It would make a great place to have a drink and snack, unwind, and delve into the material the two had printed.

After parking the Navigator, the anxious twosome entered the front door of the coffee shop. The sign reading "PLEASE SEAT YOURSELF" gave them the opportunity to choose a front window booth. It would afford them plenty of room for their research and a view of the main street in Equality. The men, not wanting to spoil one of Carla's delicious evening meals, ordered coffee and light sandwiches from the waitress named Evelyn. While they were waiting for their food, each began organizing his printouts in neat stacks. They carefully crisscrossed the papers keeping the articles in order. Both of them had been accustomed to organizing materials in their jobs.

James and Robert began sharing tidbits of information they had discovered in their search even before the server brought the beverages. A look of accomplishment adorned their faces, and the words flowed easily between the two. When Evelyn brought the sandwiches, the men hurriedly ate trying not to forget their manners in the process.

Robert proceeded to share more about the newspaper article he had found about "Uncle Bob". He began to read the text and paraphrased its contents. "Listen to this, James," Robert instructed. "The article is from a paper dated Monday, April 12, 1948. It was in the *Elgin Daily Courier-News,* Elgin, Illinois."

James interrupted his excited sidekick, "Elgin is close to Chicago, right, Robert?"

Robert responded in the affirmative and kept on reading. "The article said that Robert (Uncle Bob) Wilson died yesterday so that means he died on April 11, 1948."

"Robert," James noted, "you two share the same name. Go on; I want to hear more."

Robert continued, "It says he was 112 years old, and he had celebrated a birthday on January 13. He died at the Elgin State Hospital; he was a veteran of the Civil War, and it even tells a little about other personal history. Listen to this, James, according to the article, the War Department's records show he was not only born into slavery in Richmond, Virginia, but he had witnessed the hanging of John Brown in 1859. What do you think about that, history professor?"

James eagerly commented, "I'm all ears—read on Robert!"

Robert enthusiastically continued, "He took the name of the plantation owner where he lived." James nodded his head in agreement knowing it was a common practice among slaves to take the name of their owner. "He enlisted as a private in Company H of the 16th Regiment of Virginia Infantry on October 9, 1862, and was discharged on May 31, 1863. It also says that he later farmed and became a preacher."

"Does the article say how he got to the hospital?" James quizzed.

Robert scoured the article for more information. "No, but wait just a minute. I recall another page I read that told about how he did get there. Oh, I printed out several things; let me find that one. Here's the other article that does say that he had been living in Chicago at the time he was admitted to the Elgin State Hospital on February 14, 1941. It also states that he was found wandering the streets and taken to a hospital in Chicago and later sent to the state hospital in Elgin. Well, back to the *Elgin Daily* article, apparently the governor gave him *another* fifty-cent piece for his birthday. The governor wanted to replace the lost coin which he had given him earlier."

"Does the article give any more information we can use, Robert?" James questioned.

Robert, looking up with a slight grin on his face said, "YOU GOT IT! He is buried in the state hospital's cemetery." The two men said in unison, "Go by the cemetery on our back to Chicago!"

"Anything else in the article?" James teasingly badgered his co-investigator.

"No, not in this article, but on another printout it does state he was verified by the Illinois Veteran's Service Officer as having enlisted not as a servant or slave."

"Well," James sighed, "that tells us that he left Crenshaw's clutches sometime before 1859 or at least before October 1862, doesn't it?" James leaned forward on the table and looked Robert square in the eyes, "Robert, the information we have discovered about John Hart Crenshaw is a perfect example of the '*Reverse Underground Railroad*'! I know you remember from studying U. S. history that the Underground Railroad was a system of anti-slavery people, before 1861, who helped fugitive slaves escape to Canada and the free states."

"Sooo," Robert nodding in agreement responded, "The Reverse Underground Railroad was a system, which Crenshaw participated in, that captured fleeing slaves and returned them *to* slavery."

"That's exactly right, Robert," James replied. The two men sat in silence for several minutes as they tried to comprehend the gravity of the nature of mankind. Some risked their lives to save people from the institution of slavery while others profited by selling human beings back into slavery.

The men continued going over more information as quickly as possible. Suddenly James looked at his watch. "Robert, it's 5:30. We need to get back to the B & B before the girls begin to worry. They gathered all of their papers trying to maintain their neat order. James grabbed the check, Robert left the server a tip, and they left to meet their wives once again with more information they were eager to share.

Once back at Hickory Hill, James and Robert noticed their spouses were nowhere to be found. They decided to go up to James and Shelli's room and go over more of the information they had collected at the library. When they entered the room, James spotted a hand-written note lying on the bed. The note was from Shelli; it told the guys not to worry that they had gone shopping and looking for vintage clothing stores for Pat. "Well, it looks like the girls won't be back for a while," James relayed the message to Robert. "They decided to shop and are going to have dinner in town. It looks like we are on our own, Robert."

"Pull up a chair," James invited his research partner. "Let's take a look at more of our articles before Carla calls us for dinner." Both men began to probe the material they had printed out in the library. Some of the pages had been skimmed over, and they didn't really know for sure what they had actually printed out. They silently read all of the papers looking closely at each word in order to scrape together every tidbit of information from the black and white pages. When they found something that might be pertinent to their investigation, each man shared it with the other. Both men took notes and referenced them according to the article and page number. The research skills the two amateurs had honed over the years paid off.

All of a sudden, James jumped up quickly from his chair holding a one page printout he had overlooked. "Robert, this article came from the *Journal of the Illinois State Historical Society* on page 3 of the printout. It states, 'Wilson claimed to have fathered three hundred children with various slave women at six plantations in the South and at Crenshaw's house.'"

With every new discovery came affirmation of Mr. John's tales. Some of the old man's words may have been embellished, but most of the important information from his stories was confirmed on the printed pages and in the old journal itself.

The men were so caught up in their investigative work they didn't hear Nick come up the old oak stairs to the landing outside of James' door. He knocked quietly and told the men that dinner was being served in the dining room. "Oh, thanks, Nick, we'll be right down," James replied. The guests quickly gathered all of their papers and "salted them away" in James' briefcase. "We don't want something to happen to this research material," James warned as he spun the combination lock on the case and slipped it under the antique bed. The two were ready for the evening meal.

As Robert opened the bedroom door, the upstairs hallway was saturated with wonderful aromas coming from Carla's kitchen. Robert sniffed the air and remarked, "Mmmm, do you smell that? My mouth is watering. Hurry up! Let's eat!"

The Kansas couple was already seated at the table when James and Robert entered the dining room. Carla greeted the two men as she came through the kitchen door holding a large iron Dutch oven filled with pot roast, potatoes, carrots, and onions. "Your wives told me earlier this afternoon that they would be shopping and wouldn't be here for the evening meal."

"That's right," James confirmed Carla's statement. "Shelli left a note on our bed."

"When those two start shopping, they never know when to quit," Robert interjected.

The guests enjoyed the meal Carla had prepared and retired to the downstairs sitting room for coffee and more conversation. "How long are you guys staying at Hickory Hill?" Robert quizzed the couple.

"We don't know for sure," answered the young wife.

Nick cleared his throat and changed the subject quickly to sports news. "More coffee, anyone?" offered Carla. "I made these 'chocolate spoons'. You must try them in your coffee."

"Sure, why not?" James agreed. The guests enjoyed their evening chocolate-flavored coffee and chatted about last night's weather, current events, and the area's points of interest. James mentioned to the couple that they should explore Cave-in-Rock State Park. "It's really an interesting place," James added. His statement sparked an interest in the Millers.

"Yes, that sounds great. I think we will do just that in the morning," returned Lee.

"But don't we need to stay around here. . ." the young woman began but was cut off by Nick jumping into the conversation.

"No, you two, go ahead. Everything will be fine here," reassured Nick. James made a mental note of Nick's suspicious intervention when Shea tried to ask questions about their plans.

After everyone had finished his coffee, Pat and Shelli entered the front door of the inn. Pat called for her husband's assistance with her packages. Robert responded immediately to his wife's request for help.

Pat and Shelli excused themselves after greeting everyone and went up to their rooms.

"Well, I had better go see what Shelli has bought today. I may have to apply for a loan," James said facetiously. "I will see all of you in the morning." Nick, Carla, and the Millers bid James goodnight.

As James placed his foot on the second step of the worn staircase, Nick called after him. "Carla and I have to go into town in the morning after breakfast. I need to get some seed and fertilizer, and Carla needs to grocery shop. Is there anything we can get for any of you folks while we are in town?"

"No, thanks, I think the girls have already bought enough," James joked.

As the professor ascended the staircase, he overheard the young wife ask, "Do you think it will be tonight?" James stopped and listened for a few seconds for an answer from someone, but the conversation stopped abruptly. He continued up the stairs. The weather was certainly better tonight than it had been last night. Everyone would surely enjoy a restful sleep in the old house tonight.

Chapter 9 Secrets

James and Robert were up early the next morning. While Carla prepared breakfast, they savored an early morning cup of coffee as they sat on the large front porch. They enjoyed the view of the spring flowers and the tunes of the song birds. The friends watched robins gathering nesting materials as they hopped from one place to another. The birds were happy and carefree as they prepared for their young.

Robert said with sadness, "I hope Pat can get pregnant, James. She wants us to have a baby and soon.

She says her biological clock is ticking, and we are running out of time. I've told you about all the tests both of us have gone through, and the doctors can't find a problem with either one of us. Some of them think we are putting too much pressure on ourselves and encourage us to be patient. Pat has already thought about adoption, but I don't know if I could rear someone else's child."

James reached over and put his hand on his friend's shoulder. "Hang in there, Robert. Things will work out. I think you and Pat will make wonderful parents. Shelli and I aren't ready for a family yet. We have discussed it, and we both agree. Things will be OK; you'll see."

As the men finished their coffee, James pondered. "We need a plan to explore the attic. Do you remember last night Nick said he and Carla were going into town this morning?" Robert nodded in agreement to James' question. "Well, while they are gone, I want you to keep

Shelli and Pat busy. I'm going to do a little investigating around the house. Because of the things the girls discovered in their research, Mr. John's stories, Crenshaw's journal, and the picture Shelli took, I want to see the rooms on the third floor myself. Do you remember the part about the wagon driving into the house and the odd place on the north side of it one of us asked about on our first tour? There has to be a way up to that floor other than the sealed stairs on our floor. If there were someone in the window when the picture was taken, how did they get up there? There are strange things going on here. What happened to the girl I saw and the doctor that came last night? Remember, I told you about them? Where did they go? Robert, we have some questions that need to be answered."

Nick opened the front door as James finished his last sentence. He was startled because he didn't realize Nick had been so close. "Breakfast is ready, gentlemen. Your wives have beaten you to the table. Come on in and help yourselves."

Robert, in his usual manner answered, "I'm ready for anything. How about you, James?" Robert gave his buddy a quick wink, and the old friends left the front porch to enjoy a country breakfast.

After a savory morning meal, Carla hurriedly cleared the dishes and left with Nick to shop for groceries and other supplies. The young Kansas couple took James' suggestion and left to explore Cave-in-Rock. With everyone gone, James had time to begin his exploration of the old house. He gave the agreed upon signal to Robert to keep the girls occupied during his absence.

"Sure," came the swift reply, "but I want to go back with you if you find anything," whispered Robert.

"OK, give me an hour, and I'll report back to you if I find something."

The first task was to check the back of the house again to determine approximately where the drive-in door had been for slave deliveries. He figured a staircase would be in that vicinity. He walked around the house nonchalantly as if taking a leisurely stroll. He gazed at the countryside in appreciation of its spring beauty. Then, he slowly turned and faced the back of the house. What had aroused notice on the initial tour with Nick was now clear with the old man's description in his head. A faint outline of a large door was visible. He took note of its position and went back inside the house through the side entrance. From his observation, he assumed a staircase would lie somewhere near that door to accommodate the captured slaves.

Once inside, he entered the kitchen through the dining room. He walked around in the kitchen and storeroom. No staircase was visible. A tall cupboard was positioned outside the dining room door as if standing guard. He observed it carefully and realized the legs were about a fourth of an inch off the floor. It was attached to the wall! Upon further examination, he discovered a latch behind a stationery pitcher. That was strange! Why was a pitcher attached to the shelf? At the same instant, James solved his own puzzle. It was to hide the latch! After looking around to make sure there were no spectators, he pulled the latch. The cupboard swung open slowly and there before his eyes was a narrow staircase. The old man was right! It was just as he had said.

James felt for a light switch involuntarily, but none was found. He fumbled for a small penlight attached to his key chain. He climbed the stairs stealthily. He didn't want squeaking to betray his presence. The stairs were narrow and steep but solid. His tiny flashlight lit dark unadorned walls. His heart raced and his imagination went into overdrive. What these walls had seen in the past flashed through his head. Thoughts of escaped and recaptured slaves on their way to freedom being forced into breeding rooms played havoc in his brain. He reeled slightly and paused momentarily to steady himself against the wall before continuing his ascent.

At the top of the stairs he was almost afraid to look for fear of seeing the breeding chambers the descendant of slaves had described to him. Instead, immediately to his right he saw a door. A dim light shone under it. With his penlight, he surveyed the surrounding walls. They looked fairly new and sectioned this small area off from the remainder of the attic space. James slipped quietly over to the door. He listened for any sound that would alert him to a person occupying the room. As he pressed his ear to the door, he tried to suppress his urge to breathe faster. The light under it indicated someone must be in the room. He tapped very quietly on the door not wanting to startle anyone or call attention to his presence. He opened the door slightly. His heart began to beat faster; his palms and brow were wet with sweat. He anticipated but dreaded seeing what lay beyond the door.

Slowly and as quietly as possible, James pushed the door completely open. It was a sparsely furnished room with hospital-like furniture. In it stood a hospital bed, a metal dresser, a narrow wardrobe, a portable TV, a baby bassinet, and the window with shutters that appeared in Shelli's photo. A startled young girl looking "very" pregnant entered the room from what appeared to be a bathroom. Upon seeing James, she asked cautiously, "Are you another doctor?"

"No, I'm James Carlton; I'm a guest here. Who are you?"

"I'm Judith Owens."

"What are these rooms up here? Are you an employee?" questioned the ever curious James.

"No," replied the girl quietly.

"I'm sorry; I don't mean to pry. I'm a history professor at Northwestern, and I'm curious about the history of this house and the hidden stairway I just discovered. "

"Oh, really? I'm from Chicago," informed the young lady. She sounded happy to see someone from her home area.

"If you are not an employee, are you a guest?" continued the persistent James. Our friends, my wife and I are, but this doesn't look like a guest room."

"I'm visiting with Nick and Carla for a few days," informed the girl.

"You asked if I'm a doctor. Are you expecting one?" quizzed James.

"Yes, I am," she replied. "I'm not feeling well."

"Do doctors still make house calls in this part of the state?" questioned James.

"Yes, as a favor to Nick and Carla they do. I can't afford a hospital. Do you mind leaving my room, please? I'd like to rest for awhile. I feel very tired."

"Yes, of course, I'm sorry to barge in on you and question you like that. I hope you feel better. Are you due soon?" James could not resist one final question.

"Yes, very soon. Please forgive me, but I need to lie down now."

"Again, I'm sorry for disturbing you. Maybe I'll see you later. I'll close the door behind me."

"Thank you," responded the soon-to-be mother.

James descended the stairway with the tiny light again showing the way. He surveyed the area more closely going down and discovered a chain attached to an overhead light fixture. He quickly returned to the others still sitting on the porch. "You won't believe what I just discovered!" he blurted out in a half whisper.

"What now?" returned Shelli, accustomed to her husband's amazing discoveries. "Where have you been?"

"There IS someone in the attic! I found a hidden staircase in the kitchen. I thought I would find some evidence of the breeding rooms Mr. John told me about. There are a couple of rooms up there—at least one bedroom and a bathroom. A very pregnant young girl is up there. She said she was visiting Nick and Carla for a few days. She asked me if I were a doctor."

"So, my pictures told the truth. There WAS someone in the third floor window! I knew it was a person. I told you so," Shelli said excitedly.

"Yes, your pictures didn't lie. There is someone up there now. The room was strange, though. It looked more like a hospital room than a guest room. I wonder why she asked if I am a doctor? All that doesn't add up to a typical guest," James said. "There is something perplexing going on here, and I'm going to find out what it is," he added.

"I want to help," volunteered Robert who loved a good mystery.

"You two! What if there is nothing going on here except what she said," retorted Shelli. "Your MP experience makes you overly suspicious. Maybe she is a pregnant family friend who needs to see a doctor. That could be all there is to it. This *is* a rural area. Doctors here may still make house calls for their friends," she added trying to convince herself as well as her husband.

"I've been up at night at odd hours. There have been vehicles coming and going at strange times. Now, I discover this. I know there is something peculiar going on," insisted James.

"Your imagination could be going wild," suggested Pat. "After all, you found an old journal, and you discovered some incredible information. You may be reading more into this situation than really exists."

"You may be right, but I need to know. Robert and I are going to go back up there. I didn't find what I was looking for. There was only a small section of the attic being used for rooms. What's in the rest of the attic? And what is really going on in the part I found? I have to find out what else is upstairs," James said more to himself than to anyone else.

"Oh, James, please leave this alone. So, what if it is true? What difference does it make? We know slaves were mistreated. Why *torture yourself* with proving this old inn was a "breeding" house? This is supposed to be a relaxing retreat."

"I would think *you* would understand. It could have been our ancestors who were bred here like animals," countered James.

"I know; it *does* hurt to think of it, but that was in the past."

"No, it's still going on. There is a young woman up there who may not have had a choice but to give up her baby. I don't know; but if my suspicions are correct, she may have no other options. Her free choice to keep her child is gone possibly because of her financial bonds. Is this country still so uncaring toward its citizens that money can buy a child and lack of it can force giving up a child. The lack of freedom of choice is the common factor here even if circumstances are not as extreme as they were in the past," insisted James, always the human rights advocate.

"I know, but you can not change it! It is not our business even if what you say is true. It's a stretch to jump to that conclusion. We can not alter the past or keep Nick and Carla from taking advantage of people," reasoned his wife.

"Will you help us or not? I KNOW something is not right up there. We're going to explore that attic. I'm sorry, but I have to do this," pleaded the driven history professor.

"OK," said Shelli, "I'm curious, too, but be careful. What if Nick and Carla show up?"

"Keep them occupied as long as you can. We'll be down as quickly as possible."

"We'll do our best," the women agreed.

"Thanks," responded James quickly, "I know I can get wound up in my imagination sometimes, but I really think I'm on to something. You wait and see."

"The problem is—what if you are—what then?" Robert interjected.

"I don't know," James mumbled under his breath. "I will have to decide that later! I don't want to intrude on the girl, but I want to explore the attic area again.

Maybe there is a passage to the other part of the attic up there somewhere," James speculated.

Robert, playing Dr. Watson to James' Sherlock Holmes, slyly slipped behind James as he entered the house again and headed for the hidden staircase. "Look at this," James said quietly to Robert as they stood before the sentry cupboard, "I first noticed the cupboard is slightly off the floor; then I discovered a latch behind this pitcher. I don't want to use the light in the stairwell. We will have to use my penlight. Do you have one?"

Robert, a former Boy Scout, pulled out a mini flashlight. "I can do one better than that thing!" he said grinning broadly. "A Boy Scout is always prepared." He chuckled quietly and then slipped behind the cupboard door as he followed James up the staircase.

These two men, one black and one white, were friends, but during the years of slave trading this was not normally the case. They were college friends and continued to be close. Each had respect for the other, and prejudice was not an emotion wasted on them.

Very carefully and quietly Robert and James ascended the narrow, dark staircase. They stepped up on each step slowly and deliberately. James wondered how many slaves had been forced up these very stairs to be bred, tortured, or both. When they reached the top, the flashlights, meager as they were, found the door to the sparsely furnished room and another door across from it. James had opened it before and noticed it contained various supplies. He closed it quickly upon discovering it was a closet. This time since the walls bore no indication of an entrance to the remaining attic space, James examined the closet more closely. At the very back under the lowest shelf, there was another door that opened out from the closet.

"Look at this," James whispered in an almost inaudible tone. He motioned with the penlight focusing on the newly discovered door. "I'm going to see where this goes. You stay here and wait for me and listen for anything going on in the other room."

"No, I'm going too. Nick might show up and catch me. If he catches me, he will look for you," reasoned Robert.

James crouched low in the cramped space at the back of the closet. He opened the small homemade door and closed it after they crawled through the opening. With flashlights in hand, each investigator made his way into a larger, dark area located behind the closet. The men could stand in this area but only by bending over slightly. It was quite obvious that anyone who had to occupy this space for a long period of time would become uncomfortable. James shined his small light upward then to each side of him. He looked for any clue connecting what Mr. John had described earlier to the existing space the men found themselves exploring. Robert used his light to inspect the rough floorboards. They were old, all right! They were the old style tongue-and-groove.

A musty smell permeated the air. The men saw no source of outside light except rows of holes near where the roof and the exterior walls met. That made the holes almost invisible from the outside. The holes appeared to be drill bit holes about two inches in diameter. The rows of perforations ran parallel with the low ceiling. The holes couldn't allow in much light and very little fresh air. The openings did let in enough sunlight to reveal tiny dust particles as they floated freely in the stale air. The ceiling was built with roughly-hewn planks. As the pair continued to explore further, they found the area for which they had been searching. This opening was taller and looked as if it were at the peak of the roof of the old house. Time had taken its toll on the attic space, but evidence of the smaller rooms still remained.

James and Robert were in disbelief! Instantly, they experienced flashbacks of Mr. John's words about the breeding rooms in the attic. It was no longer *just a story* told by an old man. Here was factual evidence of the past. After James spotted the rough lumber studs, he motioned for Robert to join him. Upon inspection, it was clear the studs were used to form cubicles. Some of the wooden plank shelves, perhaps used as beds for slaves, helped form the cage-like partitions. They remained intact as if frozen in time. Cobwebs and dirt dabbers' nests were numerous on the frames of the cubicles and ceiling.

Robert's foot hit something on the floor. He shined his light down to discover several large metal rings. He leaned over to inspect his find. James knelt and gasped as he felt the worn rings, "These were used to secure chains that held this old attic's captives. I read about these in the journal."

James directed his light to what he thought was the back section of this large area. There it was! What he had dreaded finding—a large post reaching from the floor to the apex of the roof. It looked to be about twelve to fourteen inches in diameter. Upon further inspection and a little scraping with his pocketknife, he determined the wood to be cedar. That wood could stand the test of time itself. Attached to the post high above the floor was a large metal ring. What had been its purpose? Perhaps it was used to secure someone being whipped by Crenshaw's men or Crenshaw himself. Maybe it was a means of holding someone while other atrocities were going on in the attic. The post still revealed marks resembling indentations made by the end of a leather whip. James recalled similar markings from his studies of other slave stories. They observed other marks on the studs and floors of the cubicles. Were the scratches words and symbols or the etchings of desperate people?

The men walked cautiously and as quietly as possible. They were not sure as to the stability of the old floor. Both were in awe of their findings. Each man used as many of his senses as possible: sight, hearing, smell, and touch. They tried to envision the events that could have transpired here over 150 years ago. They investigated the area as quickly as they could. They knew very little time remained before Nick and Carla returned from town. They spoke in a whisper as they tried to absorb and store mentally as much of their findings as possible.

Suddenly, they heard the muffled sound of Nick's farm truck coming up the drive. James and Robert hoped their wives could keep the B & B owners from coming in the house until they could make their way out of the attic area and down the narrow stairs. The men moved quickly and as quietly as possible.

Shelli and Pat met the De Cheins as the truck came to a stop. The girls engaged their hosts in conversation about their purchases and made inquiries as to what Nick was going to plant. As the four moved toward the house, James and Robert emerged from the front door with four glasses of iced tea in hand.

Smiling and talking to their wives, James and Robert handed the glasses to the girls. James boasted proudly, "See, we can find things we look for, can't we, Robert."

"You bet we can," Robert agreed.

"How was your day in town, Nick?" James asked as he took a sip of tea.

"Oh, it was the same old thing around this part of the country," informed Nick. "See a few of the locals, talk a while, discuss spring planting, the weather, and new folks in town. By the way, someone asked me about some of my guests. I saw the librarian. She said there had been some strangers in her library the last few days. She went on to say they had been using the computers more than most of the residents. From her description, it sounded like you guys."

"Yes, Robert and I had to take care of some business even though we are on vacation. The girls were in earlier doing some e-shopping. You know how these women are; if they can't find something in a store, they go searching online," James answered evasively. Nick shook his head in total agreement. Much to James' relief, the conversation drifted to another subject.

The friends, being the gentlemen they were, assisted Carla with her grocery sacks and other purchases. Nick drove on down to the storage building to unload the bags of seed and fertilizer he had purchased. After the obliging guests carried in the last of the supplies, they couldn't wait to share their findings with their wives. "Let's go for a walk on the nature trail," suggested James.

"Sounds good to me," Robert agreed.

Carla, still in hearing distance, overheard James's suggestion. She pointed out, "The trail is beautiful this time of year. Lunch will be a little later today, so you will have plenty of time to enjoy your walk."

The hikers started down the winding trail toward the Saline River. It was a beautiful spring, but that was not the real reason for *this* walk. James and Robert needed to share their attic discoveries with their spouses. The group found a shady bench near the river, and the husbands began to divulge their findings. The wives listened in amazement to their husbands' stories. They had so many questions it was hard for the guys to answer them quickly enough. "What about the girl? Did you see or talk to her again?" Shelli quizzed.

"No," James answered, "we only explored the unfinished part of the attic. We wanted to find out as much about that area as we could before Nick and Carla came back from town. We may try to check on the girl later tonight."

The couples talked about an hour. James and Robert purged as many details from their memories as they could. They all sat in silence; then Shelli spoke. "All of this is so hard to digest at once. What started out to be a nice, fall getaway last year turned into a dark mystery. Now with another sinister discovery, there is more to be solved. I'm worried about that girl upstairs! We can't do anything about the past. If something is going on NOW, we surely must find out what it is and not let history repeat itself by standing idly by and doing nothing." The others nodded their heads in agreement.

It was time to return to the bed and breakfast for lunch. As the couples walked up the hill from the river, they viewed Hickory Hill with a much different perspective than they had last fall when the four posed for one of Shelli's photos. There was no equality on this

land near a town named Equality. Pat mentioned the
sign they had read that day "Your Peaceful and Serene
Journey to the Past". That sign had definitely *not*
become a reality for these four friends from the city.

Chapter 10   Trapped

The rest of the day dragged by as the couples awaited
the evening meal and nightfall. Everything progressed
fairly normally at dinner except Carla disappeared
several times into the kitchen after serving the main
course. Each time her disappearance was longer. Nick,
while talking to his guests, continued on in conversation
and acted as if nothing was out of the ordinary. James
tried to observe Carla and any out-of-place comments or
looks she gave Nick on her return trips. James and his
comrade detectives played along as if nothing unusual

was happening. Nick left the dining area for a short time and returned as everyone was going into the sitting room.

The after-dinner conversation drifted to the Millers' trip to Cave-in-Rock. For about an hour and a half, James and his fellow travelers pushed aside the puzzling events that were going on in the house and enjoyed discussing and reliving their trip to the state park. Shortly, Carla entered the sitting room. She asked for Nick's assistance in the kitchen. "Duty calls, ladies and gentlemen," Nick retorted. "You folks, go ahead and enjoy your evening. I'll see what my wife has 'cooked up' for me to do now."

Nick returned with details of his duties, "It was a little something Carla thought she couldn't handle by herself. One of her kitchen projects is moving slower than she had anticipated, and I may have to help speed things up a bit later. I'm sure my wife can handle almost anything," Nick boasted.

The evening hours were growing late. Shea and Lee were the first to go upstairs. The city guests retired a few minutes later. Pat and Robert went to James and Shelli's room first. The couples began discussing the unusual night's events. "I think something is going on with the girl upstairs," Shelli spoke with concern.

"I agree," concurred Pat.

The two husbands looked at each other and Robert spoke, "James, I think we need to go back to the attic after everything is quiet and check on that girl."

James agreed and the two decided on a time to meet in the hallway. It was also settled that the wives would stay together in James and Shelli's room because it had the best view of the parking lot. If *anyone* came to or left the house, the girls could observe the activity.

The agreed upon time arrived, and all was quiet in the aged house. James and Robert met as planned. They stepped lightly while descending the antique staircase to avoid squeaks from weak areas on the steps. When they made their way into the kitchen area, they easily saw the cupboard lit by the stove light. After the men silently opened the hidden passage, they climbed the narrow stairs. Muffled voices could be heard coming from the refinished attic room. James motioned to Robert to continue their ascent in complete silence.

Everything seemed to happen in slow motion. Time crawled much like James and Robert were creeping when they finally reached the top step. Both moved quietly in the direction of the small closet they had explored earlier in the day. James unlatched the large hook used to keep the closet door secure. Still using their flashlights, the men carefully opened the undersized door beneath the bottom shelf at the back of the closet and climbed through the tight opening. They believed this walled area was adjacent to the bathroom where James had seen the girl exiting. Their ears strained to hear the conversation going on in the small hospital-like room where James had first talked to the girl. They could hear talking, but they could also hear what sounded like moans of someone in pain. Was the girl in labor? Were there complications with the pregnancy? James thought there might be a problem when the girl asked if he were a doctor and said she was not feeling well. What was happening in that small room beyond the wall?

The men could distinguish two voices. It was Nick and Carla, all right. The word "doctor" was heard and was spoken in an argumentative manner. The walls, that separated the men from what was going on a short distance away, muffled the sound. It was very difficult for James and Robert to understand much of what was being said. One thing was clear! Whatever was happening did not sound normal.

They heard the door to the room open, and Nick's voice was more audible. He was having a phone conversation. "Doc, this is Nick again. Carla wanted me to call you. Judith is still in distress, and her vital signs are unstable. Her blood pressure is high, and Carla suspects this may be a breech birth. We don't need to lose this baby. Are you nearly here? We need you as quickly as possible." There was a long pause and then Nick continued, "OK, I'll tell her. Come on up as soon as you get here!"

Minutes slipped by with only the muffled moans of the girl in the throes of labor. Hurried footsteps were heard ascending the hidden stairway. The door to the room creaked quietly as someone entered. A stifled voice was heard saying, "What's her blood pressure now?"

James whispered to Robert, "That must be the doctor. I'm glad he's here!"

"Nick, hurry, we are going to need oxygen," the stranger's voice instructed.

The door to the room opened once again. A few quick steps were heard, and the closet door opened. James and Robert held their breath. Nick pulled the chain to the light fixture and retrieved the small oxygen canister and mask from the bottom shelf of the small closet. He stopped abruptly as the thought dashed through his mind that he had not unlatched the door to get in the closet. He pushed the idea aside in his rush to assist the doctor. The stowaways heard the closet door close and the latch return to its resting place. Then the door to the girl's room opened quickly. The conversation in the room was so muffled the men caught only bits and pieces of the frantic dialogue and occasional sounds of pain. The two sleuths felt helpless and fought the urge to intervene.

Robert whispered first, "James, what can we do? It sounds like this girl is in big trouble. She could die. She needs to be in a hospital. I can't just sit here and let something happen to that girl and her baby." Robert lunged toward the opening into the closet.

James caught his friend's arm, pulled him back into his crouched position, and shook his head in frustration. "I was thinking the same thing, but we aren't doctors, and there is a doctor with her. We can't reveal our presence yet. We don't actually know what's going on in there, and we could be putting not only ourselves but *the girl* in danger."

In the small third floor room, the delivery was not going well. "This baby *is* breech; I'm going to have to try to turn it," the doctor told Carla.

"What can I do, doctor?"

"Keep a check on her blood pressure and pulse. Let me know of any change. I'm going to give her an epidural now. I'll try to turn the baby, because we are not set up to do a C-section. Nick, do you have the oxygen ready? When this baby comes, it will probably have some breathing problems."

"It's right here, doc. What else can I do?"

"Keep your fingers crossed that we don't lose this girl, her baby, or both," the distraught country doctor said gravely. "I should have known as a physician we would eventually run into problems we couldn't handle here," he added remorsefully. "Have you ever thought about what we would do if any of these girls or their babies died? So far, everything has gone smoothly. Sooner or later, our luck will run out. It might be tonight."

"You're the doctor! Can't you figure out something to do?" snapped Nick anxiously.

"I think the epidural has had time to take effect," Carla urged. "Are you ready?"

"Let's see if we can get this baby turned and delivered."

The doctor proceeded to maneuver the delicate infant and began its freedom from the captivity of the girl's fragile body. The procedure went well, and the baby's small head moved through the birth canal with ease. When the baby's head and neck emerged, the umbilical cord was wrapped around its tiny neck. It was obvious the baby's oxygen supply was being hindered. Quickly, the doctor removed the cord and freed the rest of the baby's body. Carla began to syringe the mucous from the baby's mouth and nose and administer oxygen to assist the struggling infant's breathing.

The doctor cut the umbilical cord and tended to the girl's needs while Carla worked with the baby boy. The child's breathing was labored as he gasped for breath. Panic stricken, Carla held the oxygen mask closer to the baby's mouth and nostrils. She was willing to do anything to get the life-giving oxygen into his fragile lungs. Her attempts were futile. The trauma of the difficult birth and the tightness of the umbilical cord were more than his vulnerable body could bear. Carla pleaded for the doctor to hurry and assist her. She was losing this baby, and she knew it. The newborn was not breathing at all now. As the doctor finished with the mother, he took over Carla's position. With his fingers, he began administering compressions on the tiny chest. The doctor worked frantically, but to no avail. The baby never cried. Their attempt to save the infant had failed. All was silent in the small attic room in the old house.

The young girl was coherent enough to begin asking for her baby. She pleaded with Carla to give her the child, but Carla only consoled her. The girl tried to move. She wanted out of bed. As a mother, her instincts took over her actions. The doctor told Carla to give her a sedative to relieve her fear and anxiety. The injection took effect quickly, and the young mother was quiet. Her condition was stable, and the room was hushed once again.

Nick, Carla, and the doctor stood over the tiny infant's limp and lifeless body. Carla began to cry. "What are we going to do? This is the first baby we've lost!" Carla uttered.

"Give me time. I have to figure this out!" Nick barked back.

"OK, we can't lose our heads now," the doctor spoke.

Agitated, Nick agreed, "Doc, we have to really think about this. It's not like some of our experiences in 'Nam'. What has happened here will be investigated if we report this. We have got to get rid of this body and fast."

The doctor conceded but was reluctant. He had already lost his license to practice medicine because of a malpractice lawsuit. "You know my other loss was not my fault, but they won't believe this one either," the doctor said with a sigh. "This one could mean prison for ALL of us!"

"We have to get rid of the body; that's the only way!" Nick said painfully. "I wish there were something else we could do, but we CANNOT report this."

"What about the girl? We have to send her back to the city. What do you think she is going to do about our problem?" Carla quizzed.

"Nothing!" replied Nick. "When she comes to, she'll think the baby was adopted as planned. Anyway, what can she do? Tell someone she was going to sell her baby? The police won't believe that. Besides, she could have traded it for drugs or killed it herself for all they know. If there is NO body, NO crime," Nick said emphatically. "As long as no one else knows about this baby's body, nothing can be proved. I can take care of that. Doc, you make sure that girl is all right, and we get her safely back to Chicago."

"OK, Nick, but this is the last time I'm involved with this venture of yours. I know you helped me out when I needed it, but I'm still a doctor and I took an oath."

"Yeah, yeah, I know all about that oath. When we were in 'Nam', I remember you did a lot of things that weren't too ethical. What about your trading some of the medical supplies I brought your unit for drugs and other 'needs' you thought you couldn't live without?" Nick countered. The doctor shot him a piercing look but didn't respond.

James and Robert strained to hear any signs of life from the baby. No cry was heard beyond the wall. Their ears intercepted only fragments of the conversation. When they heard the word "body", it was not clear as to whether it was the girl or the baby. Since they never heard the baby cry, they surmised the infant was dead at birth or died shortly after being born.

The men sat in silence. Their muscles cramped from having to sit still in the same position for such a long time. Their bodies were drenched in perspiration, and their emotions heightened to a level of desperation they had not felt since their military days. James whispered as he looked at his watch. "It is 0500 hours. Our wives must be frantic and worried." The husbands looked at each other in disbelief. What would be their next move? When they heard the latch to the closet door go down hours ago, they didn't think much about it. They realized they were trapped unless they broke the strong latch from the door. They couldn't afford to be heard.

Robert questioned James about this predicament they had gotten themselves into. "How are we going to get out of here, James?" Robert sighed.

"Let me think!" James whispered as he buried his

head in his hands and ran thousands of bytes of information through his mind's computer. He tried to think of anything he had read from the research, what Mr. John had said, and what he had read in the old journal to help them escape. Finally, his thoughts went back to one of the entries of Crenshaw's writings. It was only a few short sentences he recalled encased deep in the annals of the journal, but it might be enough to get them out of the attic without being detected. It was worth a try. James remembered Crenshaw had revealed another way to get to the third floor. He had described a narrow, steep ladder leading from the old attic. The slave breeder had alluded to the fact that the other entrance led from his room to the third floor.

James motioned for Robert to follow him. The men moved with the quietness of a lion stalking its prey. James took Robert's flashlight and handed him the pen light. He shined the light in several directions. Suddenly his light came to rest on a spot located beyond the flooring. The outline of a square and hinges appeared between two floor joists. The dust, which had taken years to accumulate in the old attic, had obscured the opening. James put the small flashlight between his teeth. He motioned to direct Robert's attention to what appeared to be a trap door. The men used their hands to clear the dust, cobwebs, and sawdust. When James brushed away the sawdust, it triggered a memory from the journal. Crenshaw described how he had used sawdust to muffle the sounds coming from the slave quarters upstairs. The rusty handmade hinges felt cold and rough as the men wiped away the dust revealing the square nails that secured the hinges in place.

Robert pried up the small trap door. It was obvious it had not been used in years. When the heavy but maneuverable door was lifted, James shined his light downward revealing a sturdy homemade ladder attached to the wall.   It led down between the second floor walls

of the old house. Would this be the escape route for the

men or would it be their entrapment? They had no other

choice. James had to crouch and lie on his stomach to

lower his legs and body into the opening. He made his

way slowly and cautiously down the rungs of the ladder.

Robert followed. They noticed a heavy bolt lock on the

underside of the small trap door as they closed it quietly.

This meant that someone could have gone up, but anyone

trying to go down or escape the attic would have been

locked in. They stopped! The men were at the bottom of

the ladder with no where to go!

"We were lucky the trap door was not bolted,"
remarked Robert in relief.

"Shhhhhh!"

"What now?" Robert whispered.

"Did you hear that?" James asked his friend.

"Yes, it sounded like it came from the other side of this wall."

Using their lights, they examined the wall carefully. ANOTHER door! Where did it lead? They could not turn back now. It was this way out or risk being discovered in the attic. James hunkered down in the cramped space and placed his feet on the small door made of planks used for flooring. He pushed hard trying desperately not to make noise. The door did not budge! James whispered, "It feels like it is stuck, or something is against it on the other side."

"We've got to get it open. Let me try, James," Robert coaxed.

"OK, but be as quiet as possible," James agreed. Robert, being the taller of the two, could get more leverage. He tried pushing with his feet. Slowly the small door moved a tiny bit. Now an outline of light could be seen. What was its source, and what would they find on the other side? Pushing harder now, Robert gave the door one last thrust. Something heavy could be heard sliding. The last hard push moved whatever was obstructing their escape route enough that light filled the small space.

Temporarily blinded by the bright light, both men shielded their eyes. When James quickly uncovered his, there it was! He recognized the paper on the wall. It was HIS room, and the bright, morning sunlight was streaming in through the east window. On all fours, he quickly but cautiously slipped through the small opening and squeezed out from behind the heavy object. Just as his hands hit the floor in the room, he glanced up at the figure standing over him! It was Shelli! She was holding the antique reading lamp above her head ready to strike with swiftness anything that emerged from behind the heavy chest of drawers. For an instant, she did not know what was coming into that room. When she realized it was her husband, she trembled and could not speak. James stood up quickly and grabbed her wrists and took the lamp from her hands.

Suddenly, James spied Pat out of the corner of his eye. All of this took place in seconds but felt like slow motion. Pat came at him with a large vase she had picked up from the floor. Robert, right behind James, stood up just in time to stop Pat from hitting James from the back! All four suddenly realized what was happening. The couples hugged without a word. Tears of relief streamed down the wives' faces. Their husbands had escaped!

Back safely in the room, all four of the friends embraced again. James and Robert quickly closed their escape hatch and moved the heavy chest back into its original position. James looked at the chest of drawers and realized the house had a false wall like his antique box with the false bottom. This was another of

Crenshaw's means of hiding his secrets. This had been John Hart Crenshaw's room!

The girls were ecstatic to see their husbands. "We were so scared when that chest of drawers began to move!" said Shelli still visibly shaken.

Pat nodded in agreement and quizzed " Where have, you guys, been for so long?" Both of the wives had questions, but they also had some investigative information themselves.

Shelli spoke for the two, "Several hours ago a man arrived. He carried a small case like the one you said the doctor carried that night, James. Was he the doctor? Then about an hour ago, we heard what sounded like arguing coming from the front porch area and the Millers left. What's going on? Fill us in!"

James and Robert quickly related as much information to their wives as they could. The last bit of information they shared was they feared the baby was

DEAD, and Nick was going to dispose of the body. They hadn't heard anything from the girl, but felt like she was going to be OK from what few clues they gathered from the muffled conversation.

"What are WE going to do?" Shelli asked.

"Nothing right now. We are going to get a little rest and go to breakfast as if we know nothing," James answered. "I'm going to think over some things we discussed earlier and decide what our next move should be."

Pat and Robert slipped into the hall and went into their room. James slumped across the big four poster bed. He was exhausted. Shelli lay next to him rubbing the back of his neck gently, "What have we been witness to here, James?"

"From what Robert and I picked up from the conversation in the attic, we think Nick and Carla are running a "baby-selling" business out of this very house and something went terribly wrong. We are almost sure the baby was born dead or died shortly after birth. We never heard a cry. We discussed it while we were stuck upstairs for hours. That's probably what the argument was about you heard coming from the front porch. The Millers were supposed to get the baby. Who knows how much money that couple had already paid Nick and Carla, and they left with nothing. MONEY--it's all about the money!"

Shelli uttered in shock, "I don't believe this!"

"I know it sounds crazy, but what else can it be?" questioned James. "We are sure we heard Nick say he was going to dispose of a body."

"Oh, that's awful, James!" Shelli gasped.

"I know, but we have to find out as much about this as we can before we go to the authorities," James said as he buried his head in his hands once more. In the other room, Pat and Robert discussed the same things as James and his wife. It had been a long, frightening night in the old house.

Chapter 11 Gathering Evidence

The early morning hours slipped by quickly. It was time for breakfast again. The city couples showered and descended the old staircase once more. It was going to be difficult to pretend nothing had happened during the night, but it was imperative that they did not act suspiciously. Carla had prepared a continental style breakfast. She apologized for not preparing a full meal and gave the excuse of having a migraine headache during the night and was still not feeling well.

As everyone sat down after serving themselves, Shelli questioned Nick, "Where are the Millers? Are they sleeping in?"

"No," replied Nick. "They got an emergency phone call after everyone had gone to bed and had to return to

Junction City, Kansas. They don't live in that town, but that's where the emergency was. I think it was something about Lee's dad."

"We're very sorry to hear about their emergency. We enjoyed their company last night and enjoyed discussing their trip to Cave-in-Rock," said James.

"I know, but these things do happen in the bed and breakfast business," Nick replied. "What are, you folks, going to do today? Your trip is quickly coming to an end. Spring break is almost over."

"Please, don't remind us. It's back to the classroom, stock exchange, and research lab for us," Robert sighed.

"I think Pat and I are going to take a leisurely morning walk. We've noticed more blooms and new leaves on the trees in the short time we have been here," Shelli said with a smile. I might even get some more great pictures to add to my photo journal.

"The walking trail toward the river will be lovely in the morning light," Carla suggested.

"Your walk sounds good to me. I've got a little building project I'm going to take care of first thing myself," Nick informed them. "The weather is supposed to be nice this morning, but according to the forecast, rain will be moving in later this afternoon."

"I hope we don't have another bad storm like we had a few nights ago," Pat frowned.

The morning conversation drifted to other topics. The city couples went upstairs to make their plans. They had to gather as much evidence as they could before they left for Chicago. Nick was right about one thing. This spring break was almost over. The girls put on their comfortable walking shoes. Shelli grabbed her camera, and they met their husbands on the front porch.

The men decided to take a short drive on some of the local country back roads. Their real mission was to discuss what their next move should be concerning the events of last night. They insisted their wives stay on the walking path until they returned.

While driving and talking, the amateur investigators, decided to contact another college friend, Sabrina Taylor, who now worked as a detective for the Chicago Police Department. She worked in the Special Victims Unit. The kind of problem they had encountered in this rural area was similar to the cases she worked in the city. James pulled the SUV over to the side of the road and called her on his cell phone. The conversation entailed a brief description of what the men thought was going on at the bed and breakfast, their suspicions about the involvement of the doctor, the young girl, and the suspected death of the baby. Robert listened attentively as James conveyed the information to their friend.

Meanwhile, Pat and Shelli made their way down the neatly mowed walking path toward the Saline River.

The women had become familiar with most of the sights on the path. They were only a short distance from the house when they heard the sound of someone hammering. The co-workers looked at each other and remembered the events of the night and what Nick had said at breakfast. Was he building something? They quietly slipped from the path and made their way around Carla's rose garden. The spring buds were already emitting a sweet fragrance and would soon be in full bloom. The friends made their way closer to the sound of the hammer. It was coming from Nick's work shed. Moving silently now, the girls got into a position where they could observe Nick through a dirty, cracked window pane of the small structure.

He WAS building something. It looked like a small wooden box. What was it? He was standing in front of his project. Quickly he turned to reach for some nails and the project came into full view. Shelli saw it first.

She quickly put her hands over her mouth to stifle her gasp. At that moment Pat realized what Shelli had seen. They knew what Nick was working on in that small work shop. It was a COFFIN.

The girls continued to watch Nick as he went about his business like he would any other wood working project. He didn't seem tense or cautious. Luckily, he didn't look over his shoulder to see if anyone could see him. It was as if he had no connection to the outside world. Pat motioned for Shelli to step away from the window. She didn't want them to push their luck and give away their position. Neither friend wanted Nick to become suspicious about what had transpired last night. The foursome had discussed getting as much evidence as they could before leaving Hickory Hill. There wasn't much time left before they had to go back to Chicago. Spring break was over tomorrow.

Shelli and Pat slipped quietly around the side of the building and walked quickly back to the trail. They sat down on the first bench on the path. It was far enough away from the work shed that Nick would not be able to hear them talking. Both were in disbelief. They clung to each other for comfort. Both minds raced with thoughts of what the next move should be. Suddenly they heard the creaking hinges of the workshop doors and the thud of the wooden plank being dropped down into the metal brackets. Nick walked in the opposite direction from the girls. He had not noticed their presence. They continued to observe. He was carrying the homemade coffin. Where was he going? Had the baby already been placed in its wooden cocoon?

Shelli suddenly remembered her camera and unsnapped it from her belt. She took a couple of quick shots of Nick carrying the wooden box. The two amateur detectives made a split-second decision to ignore their husbands' advice and follow Nick as far as they could.   They would take the chance he would not spot them.   Pat pulled her cell phone from her jeans pocket and raised it to her ear. "I'm calling Robert," she said. Shelli quickly grabbed her arm and instructed, "We need to put our phones on silent. We can't call the guys! They told us to stay on the trail. Both insisted we wait for them," Shelli warned.

"You're right," Pat agreed. "Let's go!" The girls knew *they* must follow Nick to see where he was going to bury the body or their evidence might be lost.

Nick proceeded down a narrow path the girls had not seen on any of their exploratory ventures on the Hickory Hill estate. It was winding and hilly, but Pat and Shelli were determined not to quit now. They stayed behind Nick as far as possible trying desperately to keep him in sight. Suddenly the path went down a steep embankment. The girls held on to small trees and limbs as they descended. The path was becoming very narrow and was lined with blackberry vines. The vines were over waist high so the girls had to hold their arms up as much as possible. The briers clawed at their clothes and skin. Both women had multiple scratches, and their blood oozed from the pricks of the sharp briers. Neither of the city dwellers had experienced anything like the clinging vines, but they were determined not to lose Nick in this maze.

The path led to a small creek. The women could see where Nick had crossed. The shallow pool of water was still muddy, and his footprints could be seen on the bank across the creek. Hoping to obscure their own prints, the girls moved several yards to the right of where Nick had crossed. They eased into the cool water. The bottom was slippery with mud, but Pat and Shelli managed to keep their balance as they stepped to the other side of the little stream. Nick could no longer be heard walking through the brush. The trackers knew they must keep up with him. The path ascended another small hill. In the distance, Nick's bright red shirt could be seen. He was standing on a larger hill about a hundred yards away. They hadn't lost him.

The "spies" stepped a few feet off the almost unnoticeable path. There was very sparse foliage on the trees and bushes so the women had very little camouflage. Luckily, they had worn dark clothing for their walk, so they didn't stand out from the background of trees and vines. Suddenly, Nick stopped and looked in their direction. Had he seen them? Shelli stood beside Pat. She grabbed her by the forearm, and they quickly froze in a dead stop. They stood perfectly still. Nick was holding the wooden coffin under his left arm now. He had something else in his right hand he was using as a walking stick. It was something with a handle. He began walking toward a grove of trees and underbrush at the top of the hill. The girls decided to stay where they were and hoped they could still watch him without getting any closer. If they tried to go down the hill they were on and up the next hill, Nick was certain to spot them. The wives thought, "Where are our husbands when we need them?"

Nick took several steps into the thick trees and brush. His red shirt was still visible. He did not walk any farther into the woods. What was he doing now? Shelli could see movement, but he did not move away from them. Observing Nick's arms, the girls decided he was clearing the thick undergrowth and not digging. The slash of the briers and honeysuckle could barely be heard. They were also surrounded by honeysuckle vines themselves and knew how entangling the vines could be. The sweet perfume of the honeysuckle filled their nostrils as they stood hidden behind several small trees. Each woman clung to the tree in front of her for support.

The observers could not believe what they had just witnessed. Nick stopped thrashing the vines. He wiped his brow as he leaned his body on the handle. He began to dig with the shovel he had used as a walking stick. This was going to be the final resting place of the precious little one. Shelli removed her camera again. "I have to take a picture of this," Shelli whispered. "We may need this for evidence." She quickly set her camera to zoom and snapped several more photos.

It didn't take much time to dig the shallow grave. The tiny coffin was placed in the ground, and Nick quickly shoveled dirt to fill the rest of the hole. Suddenly, he stopped. What was going on? The women saw him as he removed his cap. Pat whispered to her friend, "What's he doing?"

Shelli looked through her camera's view finder and answered quietly, "It looks like he is paying his respects." She took two more pictures.

"We need to go back to the walking trail before he starts our way," Pat coaxed.

"You're right. We don't want him to know we saw this. We have to tell the guys what we witnessed. Come on; let's hurry!"

The girls made their way along the narrow path moving quickly and cautiously. They deliberately crossed the small creek at the same place they crossed the first time, so Nick wouldn't notice the muddy water and foot prints. The city girls got firsthand experience in tracking and hiding their own tracks as slaves had probably done on this very property.

During the time James and Robert had driven around and talked to their detective friend, Carla had busied herself. She checked on Judith in the small room on the third floor of the former slave breeding house. Some things in this world had not changed.

Carla scurried around trying to get Judith cleaned up and fed. "You know Joe will be here soon to pick you up," she informed the young girl. "The doctor said you were fine to travel. Finish your breakfast. Let's get you dressed and downstairs before our guests get back," Carla ordered.

"Is my baby all right?" the timid girl asked. "I think I remember something about the baby not being OK. I was kind of in and out last night wasn't I, Miss Carla?"

"Yes, I'm sure you were dreaming a lot of things after I gave you the sedative. Oh, you had a healthy, beautiful boy. The couple who adopted him was elated when they left with him. I know he will have a wonderful loving home. You did the right thing, darling. Believe me, Miss Carla knows about these things. Hurry up now and finish getting dressed, and I will help you get downstairs. It's getting close to lunch, and I will need to tend to my paying guests!"

The young girl sat on the side of the hospital bed and slipped on her shoes. "What happened to that nice man I saw yesterday?"

"What man?" Carla asked.

"The one I thought was the doctor."

"Child, you must have been dreaming. There hasn't been anyone up here except Nick."

"You're right, everything that happened yesterday seems like a blur." The girl continued, "You know, Miss Carla, if I had not found you on L>A>M>B, I don't know what I would have done. My father is running for political office, and my baby's father already had another girlfriend. My parents arranged for me to stay with my cousin. I was wondering what to do when I found you on the L>A>M>B website on her computer. You were my last hope. I can see now how you made everything right."

"I know, hun, we have to go on sometimes and do the best we can. Now, let's get you downstairs," Carla reassured the girl.

She slipped an envelope into Judith's light spring jacket pocket. "Here's the money Nick and I promised you. Nick and I always make good on the promises we give 'our girls'. Your baby has a good home, and you have some money to get a fresh start. You need to finish school first then find a good job. Your life will turn around. Take some advice from Miss Carla. Don't have unprotected sex again. Some of the young men you go with will not care. You take care of yourself. Don't come back here again. OK, child?"

"I won't, Miss Carla," the pale teenager agreed. The former nurse assisted the girl down the narrow stairs. Joe was already waiting in the yellow cab as usual. Carla handed him an envelope of money and told him he knew what to do. Judith slumped down in the back seat and leaned her head back. She was still weak from last night's childbirth. Her thoughts raced as she recalled some of Miss Carla's last words "Don't come back here". She nodded to herself in affirmation. The yellow cab started moving, and the girl was startled back into reality.

Judith looked out the window and spotted an SUV coming up the driveway. The vehicles met in a narrow section of the drive, and the SUV pulled over to the right and stopped to let the cab move on down the graveled lane. She looked closely at the occupants of the vehicle. It was that nice man she had met on the third floor! She had not been dreaming; he WAS real. Why was he staring at her? It seemed as though years had passed since yesterday.

"That was the girl from upstairs," James informed Robert.

"Are you sure?" Robert asked. "Would she be able to travel after what she went through last night?"

"I guess she is," James answered while continuing to look at the girl in his side view mirror. "That looks like the same yellow cab we have seen before. Wait, I can make out two numbers on the back—a 3 and an 8. Help me remember that, Robert. Nick and Carla must arrange for their young girls to be brought here by whomever was driving that cab. This operation is beginning to look more organized than we thought. We had better get on up the hill and see what our wives have been into since we left this morning. We need to tell them what Sabrina told us on the phone."

Judith was on the way back to the city. She looked back at the old house once more before the driver turned on to the highway. Her life had changed.

Robert pointed toward the house, and James drove up the drive and stopped in the parking lot. Shelli and Pat were not on the porch. They were already in the house for lunch their husbands guessed. The guys ambled up the front walk. James stopped and glanced up at the third floor window. Memories of last night's venture flooded his mind. It was difficult to imagine the things that had transpired this past week in Southern Illinois.

When the men entered the front door, the aroma of Carla's cooking filled the air. They followed their noses to the kitchen. They were all too familiar with this area of the house. They passed next to the old cupboard still standing guard over the hidden stairs to the top floor. "Something smells delicious," Robert complimented Carla.

"Lunch will be ready soon, guys," Carla advised with a shy smile. "Where are your wives? I haven't seen them since they left this morning."

"You can't tell about those two especially if Shelli got into her photography. She loses track of time quickly when she is snapping pictures," James commented.

The front door opened, and Shelli and Pat entered the hallway. They went upstairs immediately. James called to his wife, but she did not answer. "Come on, Robert, let's go see what the girls have been up to this morning," James motioned for Robert to follow.

Pat and Shelli hurried upstairs. They both needed to wash the blood from their arms. The blackberry briers had left them wounded. They quickly cleaned themselves up and changed their clothes and shoes. Their jeans had snags from the berry vines, and their shoes were wet and muddy from crossing the small creek. No one needed to see them before they had washed away the evidence of the risky mission they had undertaken that morning.

The couples met in Pat and Robert's room. The husbands and wives embraced. They were all eager to tell of the recent events. "Guys, you won't believe what Pat and I have been through this morning. We saw Nick bury a small coffin! We will fill you in with all the details after lunch. We had better get downstairs before Carla gets too inquisitive about why it is taking us so long. Honey, I am going to need your laptop when we come back upstairs."

The couples went down to the dining room for lunch as Nick entered the side door. "Hello, ladies, did you enjoy your morning walk?" Nick asked.

"Oh, we had a memorable time this morning," Pat answered candidly.

"I washed up in the work shed after I completed my little project. Let's eat! I'm starved!" Nick exclaimed cheerfully.

Nick now wearing a blue shirt went on ahead to help Carla. Pat and Shelli exchanged glances. Shelli rolled her eyes at Nick in disgust. The women barely made it through lunch while recalling what they had witnessed Nick do an hour or so ago. It was hard for them to comprehend how calm and unshaken he was after building a coffin and burying a baby on that lonely hill.

After some small talk, lunch was finally over. This was the first meal in the old house they had not enjoyed! The couples excused themselves and went back upstairs after their lunch. Shelli reminded James she needed his laptop so the foursome met in James and Shelli's room. The professor released his laptop from its case and handed it to his wife. "Carla said she wanted to see the pictures I took this morning on our walk. I need to download the pictures of Nick onto the computer. You guys are not going to believe what was captured on this memory card!"

Shelli popped the card from her digital camera and inserted it into the laptop. The computer automatically brought up the photos stored on the SD card. First, several photos of flowers and landscape appeared on the LCD screen. Suddenly, a photo appeared showing a man in a red shirt with a box under his arm. "That's Nick," Robert gasped. "I think we know what's in the box!"

They viewed the remaining pictures of Nick and his activities. The room was deathly quiet while the four focused on the computer screen and the images it revealed. Pat broke the silence, "Shelli, what are you going to do with these pictures? You know that Carla said she wanted to see them."

"I'm going to download them to the laptop and delete them from the memory card so I can show the other pictures to Carla." Shelli downloaded the pictures of Nick with the Photo Smart program, slid the memory card out, and inserted it back into her camera. She deleted Nick's pictures leaving only the innocent shots of the beautiful spring morning.

Chapter 12 The Investigation Begins

James and Robert were both shocked at what their wives had done earlier that morning. "What in the world were you two thinking following that man knowing what he was about to do. He could have killed both of you!" scolded James.

Robert agreed, "Patricia Jane, we don't know what kind of people we are dealing with. This could have been a dangerous situation if you girls had been discovered spying on Nick." Both of the girls were silent when they realized the gravity of their spontaneous actions.

After the husbands calmed down, they relayed the information obtained from their friend, Sabrina, to their wives. From the cases Sabrina had worked, she felt as if they definitely had stumbled onto a baby-selling operation in the old house. The couples discussed what they knew so far. James used his laptop to record notes on as many details the four of them could remember-- dates, times, names, and incidents. They included the out-of-state couples and the kinds of vehicles they were driving. They had not thought to write down any license plate numbers, but at the time they did not realize what inhumane scheme was taking place. Robert also reminded James to record the numbers he had seen on the cab. The couples assembled as many facts as they could. Every scrap of information was needed if justice were going to be served!

Pat drew a rough sketch of the trail she and Shelli had followed that morning and the approximate location of the baby's grave. Hopefully, it would assist the authorities in their case.

Pat remembered Carla had told her during lunch that she wanted to talk to her before she left in the morning to go back to Chicago. She could not imagine why Carla wanted to talk to *her*, but she would soon find out.

James reminded Robert there was one other thing that needed to be done before they left for the city. They had promised Mr. John one more visit. The men decided to take a quick drive into Equality that afternoon to visit the elderly gentleman. They thought it best not to discuss anything that had taken place at the old house during their stay until the authorities could conduct their own investigation.

While James and Robert called on Mr. John in town, Shelli and Pat decided to chat and have coffee with Carla downstairs. Shelli took her camera and shared her morning pictures as Carla had asked her to do earlier. "You are a great photographer, Shelli," Carla bragged.

"You have a very 'good eye'. I think that's the right term in photography talk."

"Thanks, Carla," Shelli replied. "I'm going upstairs and pack some things, so we won't have as much to do in the morning. We need to get an early start." Shelli remembered what Pat had said about Carla wanting to talk to her and thought this would give the two women the opportunity to converse. It was mysterious why Carla wanted to speak to Pat.

Shelli went upstairs, while the other two women had another cup of coffee. They exchanged small talk at first. Pat was anxious about why Carla wanted to see her. Finally, she quizzed the innkeeper, "You said you wanted to discuss something with me before we left."

"Oh, yes," Carla replied. "I couldn't help overhearing a conversation you and Shelli had earlier this week. You were talking about your difficulty in getting pregnant. I'm not too familiar with these kinds of things, but I have a niece who is pregnant and is not married. She is thinking about giving the baby up for adoption. I'm not sure about this, but my sister and I talked the other night. I told her about you and Robert. We discussed how nice you folks are, and I told her I thought you would be a wonderful couple to adopt her grandchild."

Pat was stunned at Carla's suggestion and thought to herself, "Was there really a niece or was this another baby-selling venture?"

"Of course, my niece would need to be taken care of financially. She is in her last trimester. She has medical bills, and she has college expenses. Forgive me, but I didn't think the money would be a problem with the two of you," Carla continued.

Pat, not knowing exactly what to say at this point, answered. "No, no, it wouldn't. I know couples who have been waiting for years for an opportunity like this. I can't believe you thought of Robert and me."

"Well, I think the legal paperwork can be handled. I don't know much about this kind of thing, but Nick and I have a very good friend who is a lawyer that might know. I think everything can be arranged," Carla assured her.

"I will definitely have to discuss this with my husband when he and James return. How soon do you need to know if we are interested?"

"Oh, you don't have to decide for sure before you leave. You have some time to think about it before the baby is due."

"Great, I'll talk to Robert when he gets back. This is certainly a surprise!"

Pat finished her coffee and bid Carla a good afternoon. She could hardly wait to get upstairs to share the conversation with her best friend, Shelli. She was happy in one way, but saddened by the prospect of being on the other side of this appalling *baby-selling* scheme.

Pat relayed what had transpired while she was downstairs. The girls were dumbfounded. What was going on now? Was Carla being honest about the niece or was this another part of the baby-selling business being conducted in the former slave house?

James and Robert had a good visit with Mr. John. They didn't stay long with the old gentleman, but they promised to visit again and keep in touch with their elderly friend. On their way from Equality to Hickory Hill, the men discussed some of the many events that had taken place during their spring visit to Southern Illinois. Their serene getaway to the past had become a living nightmare! What would be their next move when they returned to the city? They knew they had gathered enough evidence to justify going to the authorities when they returned to Chicago. The two men felt much better after discussing all that had taken place in the last few days with their good friend, Detective Sabrina Taylor.

Only a few miles from Hickory Hill, James slowed the SUV as he suddenly remembered a detail they had forgotten during the hectic last few days. He and Robert had talked about going back through Elgin, Illinois, on their return trip to Chicago. "Remember, Robert? We said we wanted to look up 'Uncle Bob's' grave site at the Elgin State Hospital Cemetery. I need to see that grave for myself. I know we have found some information about these people who lived many years ago, but that gravestone will bring everything into the present for me. What do you say, Robert?"

"Ok, with me. All we have to do is program the address for Elgin State Hospital Cemetery into the GPS. I'm not sure how easy the grave will be to find once we get to the cemetery."

They had more to tell the girls when they returned to the inn. Little did they know what had transpired while they were gone. More decisions would need to be made tonight.

When the men drove into Hickory Hill's long driveway, each viewed the old house with a different perspective than the first time they had seen it from a distance. Much of what they had experienced this last week could not be fully comprehended. The two friends did know one thing; they had a mission, and they were going to pursue it to the end. It was time history stopped repeating itself within the walls of the *old slave house.*

Pat and Shelli, wanting to talk to their husbands privately, met the men in the parking area. "Take us for one last drive before we head back tomorrow," Shelli requested. "We want to see the beauty of the spring sunset." The dark clouds were already gathering in the west. It wouldn't be long before the sun would be obscured.

"Hop in, girls. We don't have much good light left," Robert spoke for the driver. The couples started what they thought could be their last drive in the country for a while. Once out of sight of the old dwelling, Pat could withhold her new information no longer. She began relaying how Carla had approached her with the adoption of a so-called "pregnant niece's" baby. Pat told Robert and James the details of the conversation.

"Why did she approach you, Pat, about an adoption?" Robert sounded puzzled.

"She said that she had overheard a conversation Shelli and I had a few mornings ago. We were discussing the problems you and I have had in trying to conceive."

"That's strange, James and I had about the same conversation while we were sitting on the front porch one day. I wonder if she overheard that conversation as well? We need advice from Sabrina on how to handle this, James," Robert continued.

"What should we tell Carla, Robert?" Pat asked.

"I think we should tell her we are interested, so we can stay in contact with her on this. From what Sabrina has already advised us, she and the authorities will need a means to pursue the investigation. What do you think, James?"

"I agree totally. When we get back, Robert, you and Pat need to 'discuss' her offer and get as much information as you can. Let's contact Sabrina now. We need her advice on how to proceed."

The couples enjoyed their drive and the Southern Illinois sunset. It was beautiful. It was much like the one they had admired on their first tour of Hickory Hill months before, but this time the gloomy clouds capturing the sun's rays reminded them of the *dark days* at Crenshaw house.

The city guests anticipated their return trip to Chicago. On Sabrina's advice, Robert and Pat discussed the adoption plan with Carla after the evening meal. Nick was also present during the informal meeting. The foursome tried to act as if everything at the old inn was normal. They packed their vehicles and readied themselves for what would be their last stay at the old inn! None of the four enjoyed a restful sleep. Each in his own mind conjured up details of the past few nights and compared them to what they had learned about the atrocities in Hickory Hill's past.

The weather front had moved to the north and east of them during the night. The city dwellers awakened to a beautiful spring sunrise. All of them were anxious to start their return trip home. After a quick breakfast and last minute check of their rooms, the couples said their good-byes. It was very difficult for Pat, Robert, Shelli, and James to pretend they had a wonderful time and act as if they knew nothing of the slave house's secrets.

Pat and Shelli commandeered the BMW and the men settled for the SUV. The guys took the lead; Robert played "co-pilot" once more. Shelli did not want to stop this time and take a "last photo" as she insisted on doing at the end of their first trip. This had not been a "serene journey to the past".

Nick and Carla stood on the porch of their bed and breakfast, smiled, and waved good-bye to their guests. "How do you think this deal will pan out, Nick?"

"Oh, I think we can talk the ole doc into another job. After all, what does he do that makes him more money than this venture since his license was suspended for that malpractice suit? We had better get busy; we have new guests arriving soon."

The miles passed quickly as the occupants of the vehicles headed north. They stopped several times to rest, eat, or refuel. Their next destination was Elgin. James became more excited as the road signs directed them to the Elgin State Hospital. They had been close to "Uncle Bob's" grave all these years!

The couples had switched vehicles now. James and Shelli traveled in their SUV, and Robert and Pat drove their BMW. James felt the anticipation grow even stronger as he pulled into the drive of the cemetery. He spotted a small stone building near the entrance. The sign read "Grave site Directions". The drivers brought their vehicles to a stop in front of the neat stone structure. The city couples had lived in the Chicago area all their lives, but they had never been to Elgin much less this cemetery.

After the four hundred-mile trip, the travelers needed to stretch their legs. James immediately walked toward the door of the small building which housed the information they needed to find "Uncle Bob's" grave.

As he opened the door quietly, the late afternoon sun streamed through a small window. The sun's rays rested on a large book lying on a table in the middle of the one-room edifice. The interior of the building smelled musty. It was a smell that triggered memories of the old attic to both James and Robert. The professor began to thumb through the pages looking for Robert Wilson. The grave plots were categorized by numbers. Would they be able to find what they were seeking? They continued to look through the book. Each tried to make sense of the system. With the information they had, Wilson's name and death date of April 11, 1948, they located his grave plot number. Finally they had tangible evidence of his existence.

James pulled a small piece of paper from his shirt pocket and wrote down the plot number and directions to the grave site of Robert Wilson. The afternoon light faded quickly. They hurried to find Wilson's final resting place before dark.

They followed the directions from the book, and James drove slowly on the narrow paved paths of the old cemetery. He stopped abruptly. This was the right section. Robert stopped his vehicle close to where James parked. The curious couples began looking for the headstone. Shelli shouted to the others, "It's here!" she waved excitedly. The other three picked up their pace and joined Shelli as she squatted to observe the stone more closely. James was the first to join her. He ran his hand over the rough tombstone, feeling each letter that had been inscribed into the hard granite. He read the inscription: Robert Wilson - Civil War Veteran- Confederate Army-Died April 11, 1948 - age 112.

"Quick, Shelli, get your camera. I have to have a picture of this. The man who is buried here is a unique part of history!" James exclaimed. They all stood in amazement and gazed at this link to the past cut in stone.

After a long day's drive and a successful search for "Uncle Bob's" grave site, the weary couples left the neatly kept cemetery and headed their vehicles toward the city of Chicago. The spring day sun had disappeared beneath the horizon. The lights of the Windy City came into view. What a spring break this had been! The travelers could hardly comprehend what they had experienced in the last several days. They tried to digest the thoughts about the events, people, and information they had stored in their memories of the trip.

Finally, the familiar blinking lights on the towers atop the John Hancock building came into view. The Chicago natives wanted to drive the "Loop" and Michigan Avenue before heading north on Lake Shore Drive. Even the fast paced traffic of the busy city seemed to comfort them compared to what they had all experienced on their latest venture to the quiet countryside.

The couples said their good-byes by cell phone and reminded themselves about their plans to meet again. They had an important meeting with Detective Sabrina Taylor. James had spoken to her on the way back to Chicago, and she had taken the additional information he had given her and contacted the proper authorities. This case involved not only the cover-up of a death but interstate criminal offenses. She would be working closely with the FBI since the case also concerned girls thought to be from the Chicago area.

While Pat and Robert unloaded their BMW, James and Shelli continued north along the lake to Evanston. They were ready to get home and feel secure once more.

What had started out to be a pleasurable spring vacation ended in not only frustration and sadness but anger. This modern day atrocity must be righted. The friends were determined to see justice served.

The next few days flew by while everyone returned to work and resumed their regular schedules of business, school, and research. They met with Sabrina in her downtown office at the appointed time. With the hectic traffic outside and the grueling activity of the police station inside, James, Shelli, Robert and Pat were introduced to FBI agent Dennis Cartwright. He along with his team would be directing the investigation. First, Agent Cartwright wanted to get the couples' statements and any written information and photos they had taken. Sabrina had filled the agent in on most of what James had conveyed to her on the phone, but he had to follow protocol.

The FBI agent would be using Sabrina's office for his task force's command headquarters for this case. He had set up their "case board". As the couples went over the information once more, Agent Cartwright began to write on the white dry erase board. The names of Nick and Carla DeChein, doctors, Judith Owens, Shea and Lee Miller (Kansas), Ed and Paige Waters (South Dakota), Carla's sister and niece, the lawyer, and the cab driver all appeared in black marker. Everyone in the office stared at the board as the investigation took its first official steps.

What was needed now was a plan and strategy for their next move. Pat and Robert shared their information about the offer of the adoption. Agent Cartwright felt this would be a good place to start by keeping in touch with the DeCheins. Next, find Judith Owens. She was a vital part of this case. Cartwright had dealt with situations like this one before. The girls were always the victims even though they felt they had no other recourse and thought they were doing the right thing for their babies.

Sabrina was assigned the task of finding the girl who called herself Judith. Pat and Robert were to contact Nick and Carla. Phone conversations would be taped after permission from a Chicago judge was granted. Everything in this case MUST be carried out legally and professionally. The authorities wanted any charges in the trial to lead to a conviction of the criminals. This was a case of a modern day form of slavery—the selling of human beings.

Agent Cartwright assured the couples everything possible would be done to convict and punish the criminals in this case. The time and date was set for Pat and Robert to contact the DeCheins and confirm they wanted to adopt the baby. The authorities needed to move as quickly as possible to assure there would be no other victims in Nick and Carla's money making scheme.

Sabrina began searching for a "Judith Owens". It wasn't known if this was the girl's correct name, but it was all they had to begin their hunt. Chicago, including its surrounding suburbs, would be a lot of ground to cover since it is a heavily populated area. The search began with the school systems' records. James thought by looking at Judith, she would be high school age. The girl was a vital key in the case. If she could be found, they would get much needed information. They had to know how she was contacted and who she dealt with in the city. With any luck, they would find the out-of-state couples and uncover other information pertinent to the case.

The FBI began its search by trying to find out as much as it could about Nick and Carla DeChein and the doctor. Both men told the agent that Nick and the "mystery" doctor had some connection to the medical corps in Vietnam. They had overheard this information in the attic. Checking military records was a good beginning.

The identification of the driver of the yellow cab would also be part of the search in the case. The friends, who witnessed the cab on several occasions while they were at Hickory Hill, thought it was a Chicago cab and had luckily remembered two of its numbers. James had given the FBI agent the out-of-state couples' names and the kinds of vehicles they were driving. It was assumed their names were real and not aliases. Also, property records for Hickory Hill would be checked. Questions about when Nick and Carla purchased the property might be crucial to the case. The investigation began to take shape. Time was a precious commodity.

There were several meetings with Sabrina and the FBI Task Force over the next few days. The time was set quickly for Robert and Pat to contact Carla again about the adoption of her "niece's" baby. The call took place in Sabrina's office after all of the legal documentation had been obtained from the judge. Detective Taylor,

Robert, Agent Cartwright, and his technical team were present when Pat made the first call. The phone number of Hickory Hill was called and the recording device started as the phone was answered.

"Hello," a voice on the other end of the line greeted the caller.

"Yes, hello. Is this Carla?

"Yes, it is. To whom am I speaking?"

"This is Pat Cain from Chicago, Carla. You wanted Robert and me to get back in contact with you as soon as possible about the adoption of your niece's baby."

"Oh, yes. Good to hear from you again, Pat. Are you still interested in the adoption? I have spoken with my sister and niece since you guys left, and they are very interested in what I told them about the two of you."

"Wonderful," Pat answered. "Robert and I have been discussing the adoption every day since we got home, and we are definitely interested. Have you discussed the money issue with your sister? I suppose we will be dealing with her in this matter."

"Yes, we have talked about the money for my niece, but they want me and our lawyer friend to work out those details along with the adoption papers."

"When is your niece's baby due, Carla?"

"In about five weeks if all goes well."

"That is great! Robert and I should have no problem getting the money, making arrangements, and, oh yes, getting everything ready for the baby."

Carla told Pat that she would be in touch with her and asked for the phone numbers where she could be reached. Agent Cartwright had already anticipated this detail and handed Pat a paper with the numbers written on it that he wanted used. Pat and Robert's apartment would become one of the FBI's command posts in this investigation. The case was unfolding.

Chapter 13 The Case Builds

It took Detective Taylor only a few days to check the school records for a "Judith Owens." She had computer printouts from several school districts including the city of Chicago and surrounding suburbs. There were eight "Judith Owenses" on the list that fit the age description James had given her. Now, it was a matter of checking each address given and a personal search for every girl on the computer printouts. Sabrina worked solo in tracking down each house or apartment. She was very thorough in her search. The first six names turned up nothing. When she met the girls, she used the description James had given her and the dates he was at Hickory Hill. She compared their descriptions and where they were on those dates. Nothing so far in her search turned up the right Judith. The seventh name on the list gave a Chicago address on North Ridge Avenue.

After a scenic trip up Lake Shore Drive, Sabrina found the house address and pulled into the narrow driveway. She rang the doorbell of the house in the upper-middle class neighborhood. The older structure had been renovated to match the style of the newer town houses that had been built in the area. As Sabrina waited for someone to answer the door, she observed her surroundings. She could feel the cool breeze off Lake Michigan and hear the clicking sounds of the wheels on the tracks of the "L" train only a short distance down the street. A woman who looked to be in her late thirties answered the door.

"Hello, I'm Detective Sabrina Taylor from the Chicago Police Department," Sabrina smiled as she spoke to the woman and presented her police badge. I'm trying to locate a 'Judith Owens'. Her school record shows she lives at this address." The woman looked stunned when Sabrina asked for the girl.

"Is there a problem, officer?" asked the woman.

"Is Judith your daughter?"

"Yes, she is, but what do the police want with her? Is she in some kind of trouble?"

"I only want to see her and ask a few questions. There are several Judith Owenses in our local school systems. I have to make sure she is the right one. Is your daughter home?"

"Yes, she is. Would you like to come in, Detective?"

Sabrina went up the last step into the well-kept older home. She was invited into the tastefully decorated living room. The woman introduced herself as Stephanie Owens and asked Sabrina to make herself comfortable. Stephanie left the room and stepped back into the front foyer. "Judy," she called.

"What, Mom?" a quiet, meek voice answered.

"Would you come downstairs, please? There is someone here from the police department who would like to talk to you."

A petite, fair skinned, blonde girl descended the stairs from the second floor of the house. Sabrina was admiring a beautiful mirror over the mantel of the fireplace when she heard whispering before the mother and daughter entered the room. Detective Taylor introduced herself as the three took their seats. Sabrina remembered the description James had given her. Her first reaction when she saw Judith was, "He described this girl to a 'T'." Sabrina began to question Stephanie and Judith about where the girl had been on the dates in question. The dates James had given her corresponded to the girl's school spring break.

"Is there a problem with Judy's whereabouts, officer? Is Judy in some kind of legal trouble?"

"I assure you, Mrs. Owens, Judith is not in trouble with the law if she cooperates with our investigation. However, it is very important that she truthfully answer my questions. Judith, where were you during your spring break?"

The mother's face turned pale. Sabrina's trained eye noted the mother and daughter's body language changed from somewhat relaxed to very tense.

"Our daughter has not been living with us for a few months. Why do you want to know about those dates, Detective Taylor?"

"We have reason to believe that a Judith Owens, fitting your daughter's description, has been a victim of a "baby selling" scheme down state. Has your daughter been pregnant, Mrs. Owens?"

Stephanie swallowed hard before she answered, "Yes, yes, she has. We were afraid her pregnancy would affect my husband's campaign. She went to stay with my sister and her daughter who is also Judy's best friend. She only returned a few weeks ago at which time we took her back into our home. We have not discussed the details of her pregnancy. Was the adoption agency not legitimate, Detective Taylor?"

Judith remained quiet while her mother spoke. Her small hands were visibly shaking, and the girl was embarrassed as her eyes remained fixed on the floor. Stephanie looked at her daughter as she spoke. "Judy, do you know anything about what the officer is saying? If you know anything, you need to tell the truth."

"Yes, I was pregnant and didn't know what else to do. My parents said I should move in with my cousin who is also my best friend. I stayed with her for most of my pregnancy and went on to school and graduated. There were classes for pregnant girls like me. I didn't know what I was going to do until the day we started checking the internet on her computer."

"Is that how you found the adoption agency?" her mother questioned.

"You and Dad said you didn't want to rear another child, so I was trying to figure out what to do. Selena and I found a website named L>A>M>B (Learn About My Baby). It was a website set up for unwed mothers. You know, a site where you can go online and chat about your problems and your babies. The kind of website where you can post your picture, make comments, and blogs. After several weeks, I received an email asking when my baby was due and telling me there was help for me and my baby."

"Judith, I wasn't aware of a website. I thought your doctor helped you find an adoption agency," whispered her mother.

"Mom, I didn't know what else to do. Selena helped me decide to answer the email."

"Do you remember the email address, Judy? May I call you Judy?" Sabrina asked.

"Yes, that's what my friends call me. I'm named for my Grandmother Judith. I will never forget that email address. It was the answer to my problems and prayers. It was answers//hickoryhill@si.net ." The words "Hickory Hill" grabbed Sabrina's attention. Judith continued, "We emailed back and forth several times. The person at that address called herself Miss Carla. She said she was a nurse and the answer to my problem was putting my baby up for adoption to a wonderful, loving home." The nervous girl paused and asked timidly, "Am I in some kind of trouble?"

"No, child, YOU are not in trouble, but the people at that email address most certainly are. Mrs. Owens, would it be possible for Judy to come down to my office tomorrow and talk with FBI Agent Cartwright?" the detective asked.

Stephanie looked at her daughter. She reached over and took Judy's small hand in hers. They both nodded. "Yes, we want to help all we can," she replied as tears began to roll down her cheeks. "We should have been there for Judy all along. I know that now."

"It's OK, Mom, I did what I thought I had to do for me and my baby."

Sabrina handed Mrs. Owens her business card and told the mother and daughter what time to be at her office. She said good bye to Judy and Stephanie at the front door of the neat older home. She got into her unmarked sedan and headed for the police station.

On her way downtown, Sabrina called James at his university office. She conveyed to him she was certain she had located the girl he had met at Hickory Hill. She asked him to come to her office the next day for a positive identification. He gladly agreed. Now, how was she going to tell this sweet girl that her baby had not been adopted but was buried in a shallow grave in Southern Illinois?

The next day, Stephanie picked Judy up and drove south on Lake Shore Drive headed to the detective's office. The mother and daughter's conversation was limited to the traffic and scenery. They did not discuss Judy's lonely venture to the southern part of the state. Professor Carlton, too, was on Lake Shore Drive headed to the same destination.

James arrived at Sabrina's office first. He was greeting his friend and Agent Cartwright when he heard a familiar voice. As he turned around, he saw Judy and her mother being escorted into the detective's office by another officer. Sabrina knew by James' reaction to the voice and to the sight of the girl there was no doubt this *was* the right Judith Owens.

Sabrina had to conduct this investigation in a professional manner. Every "*i*" must be dotted and every "*t*" crossed. Nothing could be left to assumptions. Sabrina made the introductions of James and Agent Cartwright to Judy and her mother. She then turned the questioning over to the FBI agent. James waited patiently.

Judith looked at James, "You are the man I saw at Hickory Hill, aren't you? The one I asked about being another doctor. Miss Carla said I was dreaming and out of my head, but when I saw you in the driveway the day I was leaving, I knew you were real."

"Yes, Judith, I am very much real."

Agent Cartwright addressed the nervous girl, "Judith, we want you to know you are not in trouble, and you have done nothing wrong in regard to this investigation. We have reason to believe you were taken advantage of by some very shrewd and money hungry people. They take advantage of young innocent girls like you for their own greed. We would like very much for you to cooperate with us in our investigation. We need you to tell us how these people contacted you, what your contacts were here in the city, and any other information you think would help our case against these people."

"Miss Carla gave me $5,000. Am I in trouble for that?" Judy asked.

"No, not if you cooperate with the authorities," the agent assured the frail young girl.

"But my baby has already been adopted by a nice couple; that's what Miss Carla told me the morning I left Hickory Hill. She said they were so happy when they left, and my baby would have a good, loving home."

Sabrina took a deep breath before she spoke. "Judy, we have some unfortunate news about your baby. James was on the third floor of the house the night you gave birth. Your baby did not survive! We have evidence that will substantiate our belief that the man you know as Nick buried your baby the next morning." Stephanie gasped as she pulled her daughter close to her. Judy sobbed inconsolably as she clung to her mother.

"Are you telling me these people killed my grandchild?"

"No, we believe the child died of natural causes, but the death could most likely have been prevented if the birth had taken place in a hospital. The death, however, was not reported and was covered up. That is a crime," answered Agent Cartwright.

The girl continued to sob. Her mother and Sabrina tried desperately to console her. Stephanie cried, "I realize the mistake my husband and I made by telling our daughter we did not want her in our home. We helped bring about the tragic fate of our first grandchild. I feel responsible for all of this. I shudder to think about my little girl having been pregnant much less traveling all the way down state by herself and dealing with those awful people!" Stephanie added with a quaver in her voice, "What can we do to right this terrible wrong?"

"Unfortunately, we cannot help your grandchild now, but we can possibly keep other desperate girls and their babies from the same fate as Judith and her baby. We need as much information as Judy can give us," Sabrina informed Stephanie.

The young girl regained her composure. "I'll help you any way I can," she addressed Sabrina.

"You need to tell Agent Cartwright the information you gave me yesterday about the website and answer any questions he has for you."

"I'm ready, Detective Taylor."

"Why don't you call me Sabrina? I have a feeling we are going to be seeing a lot of each other for a while."

Sabrina's kind words calmed her, and Judy answered Agent Cartwright's questions. One of his assistants took notes on the large white case board in Sabrina's office while Judy's voice was being recorded.

"I was contacted by email. Miss Carla gave me an address of a doctor in Chicago who examined me several times. He was not the same doctor who delivered my baby at Hickory Hill. That was why I asked Mr. Carlton if he was another doctor. I was instructed to meet a contact driving a yellow Chicago cab at Lincoln Park Zoo. I met the cab driver; his name was Joe; that is all I know about him. I met him at the baby polar bear exhibit. I was picked up and driven to the doctor's office and later taken to Hickory Hill."

Judith gave the agents times and dates. Some of the dates coincided with the times James saw her. She was the girl who got out of the cab the night James had observed her arrival from his bedroom window. More pieces of James' puzzle fell into place. Judy continued to answer as many questions as she could and remember as many facts, times, people, and places as possible. She was going to make an excellent witness against the very people who assured her she was doing the *right* thing for herself and her baby.

The information Judy provided the authorities was extremely helpful to the ongoing investigation. Names were added to the white board in Sabrina's office. The details of the case slowly came together. Agent Cartwright assigned his assistants different people mentioned by the girl. "Brad, you track down the driver of the cab with the numbers "3" and "8" used in the transport of the girl to Southern Illinois and find the "doctor" Judy saw in the city. You can locate his office address with the help of Judy's directions."

The agent continued, "For the present time, these people will be put under close surveillance and their phones tapped. It is very important to coordinate all of these activities with the "set up" adoption plan between

Pat and Robert and the DeCheins at Hickory Hill. If the DeCheins know the others are being investigated, the case will be jeopardized. We *must* synchronize the activities of *this* investigation carefully if the people involved are to be caught and prosecuted."

Agent Cartwright assigned one of his best computer experts to investigate the internet site L>A>M>B. "Luke, I want to know as much information about the site as possible. I want these questions answered. Who set it up and when? Is it a cover for the 'baby-selling' business in the city and down state? How many girls have been contacted by the address answers//hickoryhill@si.net?"

James listened to Agent Cartwright's instructions and interjected, "All of these answers will help build the case against the people involved in this modern day form of human merchandising!"

*   *   *

Several days passed before Pat received a phone call from the Hickory Hill number. As planned, the FBI agents had camped out at the Cain's high rise apartment overlooking Lake Michigan. When the number appeared on the FBI's recording equipment's caller ID, Pat was instructed by one of the agents to answer the call.

"Hello," Pat answered.

"Is this Pat Cain?" a voice inquired.

"Yes, this is she."

"This is Carla DeChein from Hickory Hill. How are you and your husband doing?" The two women exchanged small talk about the couple's recent stay at the B & B and the progress of Pat and Shelli's research work. Since Carla was a nurse, she had expressed an interest in their DNA/cell memory project.

"Oh, we are so excited about the baby! I hope you have good news. Do you have the money information for us, Carla? You said you were going to discuss that

307

with your sister, niece, and your lawyer friend," Pat asked prompted by the FBI agent sitting only a few feet away.

"Yes, I do have good news and that information for you. We have all discussed the money to compensate my niece and pay the lawyer's fee. The amount agreed upon is $75,000.00. As I have said before, we feel the money will pay my niece's medical bills, finance her education, and help her begin a new life," Carla informed her.

The agent assisting Pat with this transaction nodded his head in the affirmative, and Pat continued the agreement. "The amount of $75,000 is a lot of money, but I'm sure Robert and I can get it. How soon do you need the money? When can we see the baby?"

An estimated date was set for the childless couple to go back to Hickory Hill to see their new baby for the first time. Carla told Pat she would keep her updated on her niece's progress.

All the planning could continue now that the authorities had an approximate date with which to work. Again, it was imperative that those involved not suspect they were being investigated. After the arrangements were made, Pat commented to the FBI agent, "How ironic, secrecy is needed to apprehend these perpetrators. It's the same as it had been in the 1800's to *protect* the person who sold slaves in the same old house."

Everyone who worked on the case put in extra effort to apprehend these modern-day slave traders—baby sellers. Technically, they were not slave traders, but these people *were* dealing in the trafficking of human beings and exploiting young mothers for their own monetary gain.

Unfortunately, the sketchy information James had given the FBI about the other two couples was of no help in the investigation. The names of the couples must have been aliases since the couples' last names and descriptions of their vehicles did not match vehicle registration data banks in Kansas or South Dakota. Fortunately, for the authorities, Nick, Carla, and Joe had used their real names.

The FBI's case board had several added facts. Pictures taken from undercover agents had been added to the adjacent cork bulletin board. They had pictures of the doctor entering and leaving his clinic, Joe's cab, and Joe meeting an unknown girl at Lincoln Park Zoo. The agents continued trying to solve the identity of the girl in the pictures.

Several days later, Brad reported to Agent Cartwright at the command post. "The doctor Judy saw in the city is Dr. Daniel Johnson, and he has an office on the west side of Chicago. We linked him to an ongoing investigation pertaining to the selling of illegal prescriptions for controlled substances. He runs a walk-in clinic and treats patients with colds, the flu, lacerations and other minor ailments. Military records show that he and Carla worked in the same medical unit in Vietnam in the late 1960's."

"Good work, Brad. Anything on the cab driver?"

"Joe, the cab driver, was a medic in that same unit. He got involved in drugs while serving "in country". When he came home, he tried school for a while. He had several jobs but kept up his drug habit. From what we learned, he is now in a drug rehab program with the help of his old friend, Dr. Johnson, who runs the clinic."

Brad continued, "Our investigation still has no information on the doctor who delivered Judy's baby at Hickory Hill. There is no indication that doctor served in the same military unit as the others. He could have been someone they met while serving in Vietnam or someone

Carla met at the different hospitals where she had been employed as a nurse."

"That's good work, Brad. Keep digging for information on the doctor at Hickory Hill. Do you know anything about the 'lawyer' Carla mentioned?" Agent Cartwright added.

"Nothing is known about the 'lawyer friend' referred to by Carla several times. It has not yet been established if that person really exists. Nick possibly could have been taking care of all of the forged documents for the so-called 'legal adoptions'. No legal state adoption papers have been filed."

"So, unknowingly, those unsuspecting couples have *not* legally adopted the children they had so 'longed for' to complete their families. They have been preyed upon by this organized band of modern day 'sellers of humans'." Cartwright shook his head in disgust.

Ean Christopher, Brad's partner on the case, added, "Nick served in a support unit. He and others in his outfit kept Dr. Johnson and Carla's medical unit supplied with generators, drugs, equipment, and any other items needed to keep the medical teams working around the clock. From information gathered from marriage records, we assume Nick and Carla got involved romantically while they were in the service and were married shortly after they came back to the states. Social Security records divulge that Carla has worked at several hospitals in the Chicago area while Nick worked in the heavy construction business for many years."

Detective Taylor's assistant, Brook, entered the room at that point and contributed the information she had uncovered in her investigation. "Police records show Carla was suspected of stealing drugs from the last hospital where she worked as a surgical nurse in the neonatal unit. She has not been charged due to the lack of evidence, but there was enough suspicion to cause her job opportunities to dwindle."

Ean added, "The FBI found proof from deed records that Nick and Carla purchased the Hickory Hill property three years ago. We know from similar investigations people running these types of schemes often choose small towns or rural areas to conduct their secretive businesses. In this case, it was the gently rolling hill country of Southern Illinois."

Agent Dennis Cartwright had Luke report what he had found out about the www.L>A>M>B.com website. "We have determined the website was created from the Hickory Hill website address. It appeared on the internet a year ago. This indicates there could have been a large number of girls contacted by Nick and Carla."

"So that means many babies could have been sold for thousands of dollars each," remarked Cartwright.

Luke continued, "Our department and other governmental agencies are beginning to investigate more internet schemes and abuses. It started out as a means for communication and information like many other 'well intentioned' ventures. However, the internet has become a playground for predators, thieves, and those looking for an easy dollar. In this case, it is a 'high-tech' form of human trafficking."

The evidence continued to build day by day. Nick and Carla's operation had been carried on with a military-type objective--find young, frightened, pregnant girls; prey on wealthy, desperate, childless couples; and exploit the situation of each.

"There are no records indicating that Nick and Carla ever had children of their own. Carla seemed to be the contact person. Using website addresses, several girls in the Chicago area have been located and identified by our agents," Luke informed the group.

Brook, laying a case file on the desk, proceeded with her findings, "Profiles the bureau have worked on before show women such as Carla sometimes feel the need to help other childless women. They actually think what they do is in some way helping the girls and the childless couples. There is one big problem with this kind of rationale--they are "selling babies" for their own monetary gain, and they are breaking the law."

Agent Cartwright looked at the added pictures on the board and spoke philosophically, "When there is a market for a product, even human lives, someone will try to cash in on the demand."

Pat spoke to Carla several more times by phone. The date Pat and Robert were to pick up their new baby drew closer. Cartwright and his agents wrapped up the details of the "stake-out" at Hickory Hill. They monitored Joe's yellow cab's activity closely. The authorities felt confident the pregnant girl who had been photographed with Joe at several locations was *the* girl who would deliver the baby for Pat and Robert's so-called adoption. The investigation had established that Carla had NO sister and NO niece.

At the next meeting of the agents, Sabrina updated the group, "Judy's information told us how the deliveries of the babies were arranged. After Carla's initial contact and the first clinic appointment, the doctor in Chicago determined how many weeks into the pregnancy each girl was. He then calculated the best dates for delivery. The fixed date would be arranged for Joe to pick the girl up at the clinic and drive her to Hickory Hill. On the selected date, labor would be induced. The still unidentified doctor would then be responsible for the delivery."

Cartwright informed his team of the plan, "If Joe's yellow cab leaves Chicago in the next couple of days headed for Southern Illinois, the stake-outs will have paid off. The 'sting' operation will begin at that point. We will bring the modern day traffickers in human beings to justice!"

He continued, "Each mile the cab travels will be monitored. Every piece of modern surveillance equipment we need will be used in this operation. A tracking device has been well hidden on the underside of the yellow cab. Fully equipped satellite-tracking vans will track its every turn."

Sabrina remembered James' story about John Hart Crenshaw and the Old Slave House and shared her thoughts with the others, "Haven't we come a long way! Proof of the movement of Crenshaw's victims eluded the authorities in the 1800's. Using today's state-of-the-art equipment, we can easily track the cab's human cargo. Almost instantly its progress and location can be beamed back to us via satellite."

A few days later, Pat received the final call from Carla. The date Pat and the authorities had been so patiently waiting for was set. It was June 1. Only two days away! Agent Cartwright gave the orders for the operation named "Little Lamb" to be activated. That meant Joe's cab would be leaving Chicago for Southern Illinois. Unmarked cars and vans would be placed in strategic places along the route. Surveillance of Hickory Hill would be stepped up, and the two city couples would be making their preparations to visit the house on the hill one last time.

As was suspected, the unidentified pregnant girl arrived by city bus to Dr. Johnson's clinic early the next morning. The agents kept the office under surveillance and watched closely for Joe's yellow cab to arrive. Right on schedule, Joe pulled up at 8:30 A.M. He went into the clinic and came out escorting the young girl and carrying her small overnight bag. An unmarked car followed the cab until it reached Interstate 57 heading south. At that point another unmarked car took over and followed the cab as planned. At different intervals, other official vehicles kept the cab under surveillance even though the cab had a tracking device planted on its undercarriage. The authorities did not want to rely completely on modern-day technology.

Plans were finalized with Pat, Robert, and their two best friends who were going with them to Hickory Hill. It was agreed that Robert and Pat would wear voice transmitters when they arrived at their destination. Those would be placed on the couple before reaching the original slave breeder's home. A command post had been set up in a large motor coach in an RV park located on the Saline River only a few miles from Hickory Hill. This area was close to Half Moon Lick where John Hart Crenshaw's captured slave workers had routed flumes.

The flumes carried water richly impregnated with salt to the boiling pots that made Crenshaw rich.

Ch. 14 Dark Days End at Crenshaw House

It was a beautiful morning on the last day of May in Chicago. The longtime friends made their final preparations for their last trip to Hickory Hill. Even though the sun was shining brightly, the mission overshadowed the couples' good memories of their first visit to the old inn. Everyone realized the importance of the task at hand but were saddened by the fact that mankind had not risen above the same evil schemes to enslave. Enslavement by fear had gone on in Crenshaw's day and was still happening today. It was time for the old house to be set free from the atrocities that had been held captive within its walls.

James and Shelli picked up their old friends once again in the Navigator. They had to have room for an infant car seat and baby supplies. Everything must look as though they were actually there to pick up a baby. Pat looked at the car seat with sadness and wished it were not a prop for their mission. "Maybe we can buy one of these seats for real one day," she said halfway to herself and halfway to Robert.

"Huh?" Robert muttered in reply not knowing what she said.

"Oh, nothing, I was just thinking out loud," she explained.

The atmosphere in the vehicle was somber. The college friends carried on some small talk to pass the time. Their minds were on the impending challenge of bringing the dark days of Crenshaw House to an end. Neither woman had ever worked with the police before. They were unsure of their ability to "pull off" their parts in the operation "Little Lamb". The men, however, drew from their military police experience and felt more confident in the task ahead. The miles to Southern Illinois slipped by quickly as no stops were planned for shopping and comfort food. Fuel, restrooms, and fast food were this trip's only stops.

Agent Cartwright wanted to meet with the couples for briefing late that afternoon. The authorities' RV motor coach parked on the Saline River would be their overnight accommodations. While the couples had been traveling, surveillance had continued as planned on the old house, the cab, and the doctors.

The authorities had men posing as local electric company workers posted at a utility pole about one-tenth mile from the entrance to the driveway at Hickory Hill. They had observed a car driven by a man who looked to be in his middle to late sixties going to and leaving the old inn. The car's license plate was registered to a Dr. Shawn Michaels. When a check was run on the doctor's license plate number, another piece of the puzzle was filled in. Dr. Michaels' military and social security records showed he had served in Vietnam the same time Nick and Carla were there. He had been in another medical unit Nick's outfit had supplied. He had also later worked with Carla at a hospital in the Chicago area. The information further revealed he had lost his license to practice medicine due to a malpractice suit. He had misdiagnosed a young child who later died from complications of his prescribed treatment.

Sabrina accompanied the FBI agents to Southern Illinois. She would also attend the briefing. Sabrina would play the role of a long-time lawyer friend from college. She would pose as legal counsel for Pat and Robert although her actual purpose was for the couples' protection should anything go awry.

When the foursome arrived at the RV command post late that afternoon, Agent Cartwright and Sabrina were ready to start the briefings. The agent began, "The first thing we need to do, Pat, is call Carla and tell her you will arrive at Hickory Hill in the morning. Tell her you are spending the night on the road. That gives us tonight to go over the details and possible scenarios. Robert, will you please bring in the car seat; one of our technicians will be installing the camera and sound transmitting equipment."

Sabrina explained her role in the operation, "Robert, you introduce me to Nick and Carla as a college friend who has legal experience with adoptions. He will undoubtedly be surprised, but don't worry, I have a plan. My real purpose is to protect all of you and the baby. We don't know how desperate or how violent these people are. As of yet, we aren't aware of any aggressive behavior on their part, but we want to be prepared. They may become suspicious and panic."

Agent Cartwright filled the couples in on the latest developments in the case. "Joe, the cab driver, has been arrested on his way back to Chicago. We staged a routine traffic check under the pretense of checking registration, valid driver's license, and proof of insurance so he would not be suspicious and alert Nick and Carla. He was arrested. His arrest is just one in this baby-selling scheme."

Restful sleep eluded the team that night. Early the next morning, the five college friends were wired for recording the transaction of the baby purchase. A hidden camera and a sound recording device had been installed in the infant carrier seat. It had been made to look like part of the seat itself.

Sabrina updated the others. "The two doctors have already been taken into custody. Judith has identified the picture of the one here as being the doctor who delivered her baby. He was arrested at his home in Gallatin County for practicing medicine without a license and other charges relating to the investigation." The case against these modern-day brokers of human beings was coming fast to a close.

The Southern Illinois weather was cloudy and dark as they arrived at Hickory Hill around 8 A.M. June 1 as planned. The baby had been born in the late hours on May 31 according to what the doctor had told the authorities upon his arrest a couple of hours after he delivered the baby.

Sabrina told the friends as they were driving to Hickory Hill, "The doctor was concerned for the girl and was insistent that she be given the proper care. Agent Cartwright and I reassured him that if medical attention were needed for the girl, her health and the health of the infant would be top priority. The girl had a slight fever, and Dr. Michaels told Carla to keep a check on the mother. He promised he would be back to check on her late today. He was going to send his patient back to

Chicago if her temperature returned to normal. He was sure she would be well enough to travel in a day or two."

Nick and Carla met the couples and Detective Taylor at the front door. Robert introduced Sabrina, "This is our friend, Sabrina Taylor. She has come along to give us legal counsel. We hope you don't mind," Robert informed Nick.

"Why do you need her? Don't you trust us?" Nick angrily confronted Robert.

Sabrina quickly defused the situation by assuring Nick, "I am here as a friend and not as 'legal counsel' IF you know what I mean." The wink and quick toss of her head relaxed Nick enough to proceed with the conversation.

Carla quickly changed the subject by announcing, "I have 'good' news and 'bad' news." The foursome and Sabrina tensed at the 'good news/bad news' announcement.

Carla felt she had to make this adoption work since it was she who had approached Pat with the idea of adoption in person. She had gone against Nick's rule about using internet contact only.

The authorities, listening to every word of the conversation, were frantic trying to ready themselves for their next move. Carla continued, "Pat, you will be happy to know that the baby came earlier than expected, and you can take the child this morning. The bad news is the child is a boy, and I know you had your heart set on a girl." Everyone was relieved that the "bad" news was not really bad, and the group laughed at the joke.

Carla, still smiling, left the group in the sitting room to get the baby. Nick picked up the conversation at this point. "Carla's niece gave birth at a nearby hospital. Her mother thought it best if I take care of the paperwork and the money. She does not think it is a good idea for her or her daughter to be present for the finalization of the adoption."

Carla entered the room a few moments later with the sleeping baby boy. She placed him in Pat's arms gently. Pat began to cry. "He's precious. He's just beautiful. Are you sure your niece can give him up?" Carla helped Pat place the still sleeping child in the infant carrier. They straightened up the blanket on the tiny boy. Carla's hand came very close to the hidden camera and the couples became edgy for a few moments.

Nick pulled some papers from one of the writing desk's drawers. The papers were neatly typed and seemed to be in order. Sabrina glanced over the document's pages and quickly gave them to the new couple to sign. Robert slipped several thick envelopes from his jacket pocket. They contained a sum of $75,000 in $100 bills as Carla had previously instructed.

Robert handed Nick the money, and Nick handed Robert the papers. The deal was done!

While the transaction was taking place inside the old house, Agent Cartwright maneuvered his men outside the inn. As soon as the business deal was final, the authorities would make their much awaited move. Everything would be coordinated to the second. With the listening and recording devices, Agent Cartwright would know exactly when to send his men in.

As soon as Robert and Nick exchanged the money and the papers, the FBI agents stormed in the front, side, and back doors of the house with their weapons drawn. "Nick and Carla DeChein, you are under arrest for operating an illegal baby-selling business and the failure to report a death. You have the right to. . ." Agent Cartwright continued to quote the Miranda rights.

"What's going on?" yelled Nick.

As handcuffs clicked, Carla cried out, "We were trying to help you! Don't you want a baby? This child would have no chance with a homeless mother! We were trying to help childless couples have a family! We are helping everyone have a better life!"

"What you are doing is illegal. You are selling babies. You are lining your own pockets. You are the ones getting the most out of these deals," interjected Sabrina.

"No, no," insisted Carla. "We have to make some money so we can buy supplies and pay for transportation and doctors. We're not hurting anybody. Everyone benefits."

"Did the baby Nick buried in the woods benefit?" Agent Cartwright demanded.

Carla started sobbing and Nick hung his head. "We did all we could to save that baby. It's the only time we lost one. It wasn't our fault," protested Nick.

"We'll see if a judge and jury will believe that," Agent Cartwright said as he motioned for the officers to escort Nick and Carla outside. The two still professed their innocence as they left the room. Each step of the arrest was carried out according to the authorities' careful plan. They did not want the case dismissed and these perpetrators to be set free due to a technicality.

The sitting room where the couples had exchanged small talk and laughed only a few weeks ago looked like a sound stage for a TV detective series, but this was no sound stage. This was for real.

Pat and Shelli stood shaking. James and Robert rushed to their sides to comfort them. Everything happened so quickly. The weeks of planning had gone flawlessly. Quickly, Child Protective Services emerged through the front door and swept the still sleeping infant out of the house. Pat, having seen a baby that could have been hers, cried inconsolably. "It's not fair; it's not fair," Pat began repeating over and over in a barely audible whisper.

Agents began searching every room downstairs. James and Robert showed Agent Cartwright the hidden staircase which led to the third floor. Paramedics quickly followed Illinois State Police officers whose guns were drawn. They made their way quickly up the steps James and Robert had crept up weeks ago. It was not known for sure whether the girl was still upstairs like Judith had been. It was suspected she was still there since surveillance had not seen her leave Hickory Hill, and the doctor had told them she had a fever. He was scheduled to see her in the afternoon.

The girl was there, in that lonely third floor room, quietly sleeping after giving birth. She was startled when the paramedics awakened her. One of the female officers reassured her she was going to be all right. The paramedics gave her a quick exam and started an IV.

They had to physically carry the girl down the steps. The old hidden staircase had not been designed to accommodate a modern-day medical stretcher. As soon as everyone knew the girl and the baby were all right, the search for all other evidence that might pertain to the case began. The dark days at Crenshaw House had ended.

Records, papers, computers, medical equipment and supplies were gathered and processed. If the authorities' suspicions were correct, the bed and breakfast had been a front to launder the baby-selling business' money. Sabrina and Agent Cartwright personally supervised every detail to bring to justice the baby sellers. Agents searched the grounds and second floor of the old house first. Every drawer, closet, and cabinet were opened and inspected. Papers were boxed to be sorted and studied later. Officers began searching every inch of the third floor. The police photographer took several pictures of the hospital-like room and the hidden staircase.

James and Robert took Agent Cartwright to the second floor and showed him the secret door and their escape route which had led them from the third floor to the bedroom. Cartwright gave the orders for the officers to ascend the narrow ladder into the attic. With large, bright flashlights, the officers began to probe every dark corner and crevice of the space. The search was barren except for a small wooden trunk hidden deep in the crawl space between the roof and the old floor in the northwest corner. After a thorough examination of the attic space, Cartwright had the officers take the old trunk down into the sitting room. The emotions ran so high no one noticed the presence of the antique trunk.

Robert, James, Shelli, and Sabrina stood around Pat trying to console her. Finally, an officer approached,

"Would you, ladies and gentlemen, please accompany me outside. Agent Cartwright wants to talk to you."

Once they were on the porch, Cartwright signaled for them to come around to the side of the house. "I know this is difficult for you, but we need you to show us where the trail starts to the burial site of Judith's baby. We have the map you drew for us, but it would be faster if you could lead the way." The girls agreed to the request. They changed clothes and shoes quickly then guided the officers down the path toward the lonely grave. They once again waded through the entangled briers and bushes which were even higher now with the warmer weather growth. The somber group crossed the small creek as the girls had done before and went up the same small hill. James and Robert had some idea now what their wives had experienced the day they had followed Nick. They came to a dead stop. They looked across the narrow valley and pointed to the tree-lined hill on the other side. "It's there in the little clearing in that clump of trees," Pat pointed.

Robert hugged Pat gently and said softly, "Why don't, you girls, go back to the house and wait for us there." James nodded in agreement.

Agent Cartwright, a police photographer, an officer commanding a cadaver dog on a leash, and other officers led the procession. James and Robert followed. When they reached the top of the hill, there was no evidence of Nick's thrashing bushes and vines. It didn't take long for the dog to pick up the scent for which he had been trained. The agent directed the officers to begin uncovering vines and looking for the burial place of Judith's baby.

The grave was shallow. The police photographer snapped several pictures of the grave site being uncovered. The small homemade casket was lifted from the narrow grave and laid softly on top of the vines. The coffin was opened and the smell of death permeated the air. The decaying body was inspected by the coroner. He identified the remains as a newborn infant boy. A new, soft, white blanket was draped over the body before it was carefully placed in a body bag. The homemade coffin would be labeled as evidence. The camera's shutter clicked many times as sounds, sights, words, and pictures raced through James and Robert's heads. They were both remorseful they had not been able to do anything to intervene from their attic hiding place.

The friends stood to one side of the grave and tried to stay out of the way. As James stepped backward, he stumbled over something that lay beneath the entangled vines. He was curious and borrowed one of the officer's shovels. "I think I have found something here," he shouted toward Robert and the officers. "It may be another grave! Who knows how many they lost. We don't know Nick told the truth when he said Judith's baby was the only one who did not survive." James began to hack away at the dead and living briers and honeysuckle vines. Suddenly, the metal shovel hit something solid. Squatting on the ground, he and Robert began to pull at the remaining vines and what looked like years of rotted vegetation. James' hand felt something cold and lifeless. Whatever it was, it was covered with dark, rich soil.

For a moment the object reminded him of the rough texture of "Uncle Bob's" tombstone at the old cemetery in Elgin. The two men, oblivious to their surroundings and the activities of the authorities, scratched meticulously around the object. Its rectangular shape began to emerge from the black soil. "It IS a tombstone!" James uttered in amazement. Wiping furiously now, James rubbed even harder at the stone's surface. He could feel the outline of letters, but the grooves were filled in with dirt. "This has been here a long time," James added, still clawing at the stone. He reached next to him and broke a young locust tree sapling into two pieces. He chose the one with the sharpest point and began scraping the dirt out of the chiseled grooves. "Ouch!" he yelled startling Robert and the others. "Sorry, one of the thorns stuck in my thumb." Robert saw the bright, red blood ooze from James' hand as he picked up the other piece of locust sapling and began to help his friend. When they were finished, James and Robert sat on the ground next to the time-worn stone. Their eyes were fixed on the inscription. James read it aloud "MY BELOVED HUSBAND-JOHN HART CRENSHAW-BORN 1797-DIED 1871". The men sat in silence.

Suddenly, Robert and James were bolted back to reality by a loud voice. It was Agent Cartwright giving orders to his men, "Wrap everything up. Let's head back to the house. I'll send out a crew tomorrow to search the grounds further, but the dog hasn't found anything else. One old and one new grave is discovery enough for today. This may be an old graveyard, but there doesn't seem to be any other recently buried bodies here." The men went on ahead of the officers after James asked Agent Cartwright for a photo of Crenshaw's gravestone. The picture was taken.

The girls had heeded their husbands' suggestion and had already returned to the house because they did not want to see the body exhumed. They were in the sitting room with Sabrina when the men came in. The room buzzed with information. The sounds of papers and other evidence being boxed and readied to transport back to Chicago filled the house. Outside, every building was searched. They found Nick's old red shirt still hanging in his work shed. It had tiny visible spots which could be blood from afterbirth. It was bagged and tagged to be processed in the crime lab. The spots would be tested for blood type and possible tissue samples for matching DNA.

When James and Robert entered the room, their wives could tell by the expressions on their husbands' faces something strange had taken place on the hill "What happened? Did you find the baby's body?" asked Pat.

"Yes, we found it. It didn't take the dog long to pick up the scent," Agent Cartwright replied.

"We found more than one grave!" added James.

"What do you mean? Did you find more babies' bodies?" quizzed Pat.

"No," Robert answered his wife. "We found Crenshaw's grave and headstone!"

"Crenshaw? That's the man you told me built this house and owned the slaves," exclaimed Sabrina.

"Yes, he was buried on the land he coveted so much." The couples sat in silence as they reflected on some of the passages James had shared with them from the weathered journal he had found in the antique wooden box.

Two computers, boxes of papers, and other evidence were loaded into the authorities' vehicles. Now only one object remained on the floor where all the evidence boxes had sat—the old wooden trunk brought down from the attic. Agent Cartwright pointed and asked, "Has anyone gone through the material in this?" All eyes turned to the trunk. They speculated about the secrets held captive in the wooden vault.

One of the officers answered as he exited the sitting room door, "Yes, I checked through the old stuff. Nothing of any importance to this case. I found some old pictures and letters. Nothing we need."

Agent Cartwright turned to James and said, "You are the history professor here. It looks like it's all yours."

James sat on the floor beside the antique. "Well, wooden trunk, what treasure do you hold for us? You're the second wooden box to hold secrets from the past. Do you know anything about this old house?" James smiled as he addressed the trunk. He noticed his audience was smiling, too, at his personification of the box.

It was not a large trunk. The edges were outlined with metal. Its handles were made from worn, cracked leather. There was a lock, but the key was missing. It opened easily. The rusty hinges began to groan as James opened it carefully. He lowered the lid of the antique trunk all the way down revealing old photographs and papers. Gently, he began sifting though the articles that time had forgotten. There were several handwritten letters. One in particular caught James' eye. He reached into the trunk and retrieved a yellowed envelope.

"Look at that old stamp," Robert said excitedly as he reached for the envelope. "It looks like an 1857 or an 1858 one cent Benjamin Franklin. I have one like it in my stamp collection. See, it's perforated. Those years were about the time the U. S. Postal Service started producing perforated stamps. The earlier ones had to be cut with scissors."

"My, aren't you the philatelist?" Pat bragged on her husband.

"Thanks, honey," Robert answered as he patted his wife's hand. "James isn't the only one here who knows a little history."

Everyone's mood lightened for the first time since they had left Chicago. Robert handed the envelope back to his friend for further inspection. James focused on the handwriting and stared in disbelief. "I can't believe this! Look! It's addressed to John Hart Crenshaw, Equality, Illinois, from A. Lincoln, Springfield, Illinois." James could hardly contain his excitement. He carefully removed the faded letter from its musty shroud. The ink had faded over the years.   Its penned words were barely

legible. James read it aloud:

September 26, 1858

Dear Mr. Crenshaw,

I write these words to express my profound gratitude for your hospitality during my stay at your beautiful estate, Hickory Hill. I found your accommodations and food most refreshing to this trail worn politician. Please convey my sincere thanks to your lovely wife, Sina, for all she did to make my stay in the southern part of Illinois as pleasant as possible.

I feel compelled to pose one question to you, however, Mr. Crenshaw. Do you feel the treatment of your fellowman will be judged someday by God Himself? I most certainly *believe we will be held accountable for how we have treated each and every person we encounter on this earth regardless of social standing, wealth, or color of his skin. I implore you as a fellow citizen of this great state and country to reconsider the treatment and fate of those under your care and leadership.*

Yours truly,
A. Lincoln

When James finished reading the aged, worn letter, tears ran down his cheeks. "I have heard the stories and read the articles about Lincoln's visit to this house, but this is tangible proof. I am holding papers that Abraham Lincoln, the Great Emancipator, held so many years ago!" James exclaimed fervently. "This letter is very valuable to a collector. It might sell for thousands of dollars on eBay or at an auction. I think it should be donated to a museum in Springfield. "

Pat spoke, "That is wonderful! I still can't believe the events that are transpiring at this very moment." All four began carefully sorting through historical contents of the trunk.

Writing on the back of one photograph caught Shelli's "photographer's eye". She read the inscription aloud, "House Help, Uncle Bob, and Abigail-Hickory Hill Estate. I know these names from the journal entries," she cried out as she handed the worn picture to James without turning it over.

As her husband looked at the photograph side, his eyes stared at it for a moment; he looked up at his beautiful wife Shelli and silently passed the picture to Robert. "Are my eyes deceiving me? Tell me who you see in this picture."

Robert's face paled as he turned the picture toward Shelli and Pat. They knew something else strange was taking place at the old house. The image of Abigail, the Negro slave who had supposedly been pregnant with Crenshaw's baby when she was sent away, could have been Shelli's twin sister. An eerie silence fell over the sitting room. This slave must be an ancestor in Shelli's family. She was sent away but survived.

James, Robert, and their wives were some of the last people to leave. The men carried the old trunk Agent Cartwright had let James scrutinize. The authorities put finishing touches on the crime scene. The yellow and black crime scene tape was stretched across all the doors of the sinister estate. As the four walked out on the large front porch of the inn, the clouds had dissipated, and the sun shone brightly. It had turned out to be a good day on the side of justice.

Robert spoke, "I know it's getting late, but I think we should go by Mr. John's house before we leave. We promised him we would inform him of any new information we found the last time we saw him. What do, you guys, think?"

"I think that's a great idea, Robert," his wife agreed. "How about you, Shelli?"

"I would love to meet the gentleman. It's going to be late when we get back to the city anyway. What's another hour or two? Let's go," Shelli replied enthusiastically.

James agreed to the decision, and the four headed toward Equality. The atmosphere inside the SUV was lively. Everyone rehashed the happenings of the day. Each shared his or her thoughts and feelings about what had been accomplished on THIS trip to Hickory Hill.

The subject of the photograph of the Negro slave, Abigail, came up. "Shelli, I can't believe how much you look like Abigail!" Pat reiterated. "I wonder if you are a descendant."

Shelli replied, "I don't know. Not much is known about my ancestors prior to the late 1800's. It is so creepy! Remember when I first arrived at Hickory Hill, James asked if I had a feeling of déjà vu when I saw Crenshaw's house."

Pat answered, "Yes, I remember. You remarked about that several times."

"You know, our research in cell memory came to mind. Could that feeling possibly have been handed down in DNA from Abigail? It could be the substantiating evidence we've been looking for to prove our research theory," Shelli pondered. No conclusions were reached.

The small town of Equality came quickly into view. The friends drove down the quaint, tree-lined street.

They turned into Mr. John's driveway. He was on the front porch enjoying the early evening sun.

Mr. Wilkes perked up as he saw his friends get out of the Navigator. He greeted them as he rose from the swing. "I can't believe these tired old eyes. I'm so glad to see, you boys," he said as he looked at James and Robert. "Who are these pretty, young gals you got with you?" he directed his question to James.

"Mr. John, this is my wife, Shelli, and Robert's wife, Pat. We promised we would keep you posted on anything we found out about Hickory Hill. We just came from there. Mr. John, we have much news to share with you."

The elderly gentleman sat in amazement as the couples told their stories. They tried to give their new friend as much information as they thought he could comprehend. Their story went on for over an hour as they sat on the neat front porch and visited.

"My, my," exclaimed Mr. John. "You young folk sure has been busy. I knowed something strange was going on over there. We local people knows when things ain't just right. I'm so glad you thought about me before you left to go back up North. I sure do appreciate it."

As everyone got up to leave, Pat and Shelli both doted on the elderly man. They could tell he was lonely. "You all come back to see me, you hear?" Mr. John said with a smile on his face. "You don't know how much I appreciate your visit and that you thought about me," he repeated himself.

His feet shuffled as he walked to the front steps with his guests. James was the last person to leave. Mr. John laid his hand on James' shoulder as he spoke, "Son, you and your friends did a mighty good deed down here. I believe my old bones will rest better tonight knowing you young folk do care about not only what bad things went on in the past but about the future. Thank you."

"You're welcome, Mr. John," answered James. "We'll never forget you. You can count on that."

Mr. John watched the young couples until their vehicle was out of sight. He hooked his screen door. It was evident Mr. John had once been taller in stature. His body was slightly bent under his years of hard work as he slowly closed his front door and turned on a small reading lamp by his favorite chair. The old gentleman spoke, "Thank you, Lord, for a *good* day."

The SUV and its occupants headed for the interstate. The four lane would return them to the city they knew so well. They would soon be back in their comfort zone, and the sights and sounds of the country would give way to the traffic lights, horns, and sirens of the bustling metropolis. Pat and Shelli dozed in the back seat. Their bodies twitched now and then as each one's dreams took her back to the day's events.

James and Robert carried on a conversation and discussed the meeting Agent Cartwright and Sabrina had already scheduled with the couples on June 7. The meeting would take place in the Federal Prosecutor's Office. The four, along with Judith and Sabrina, would be vital witnesses in the case against the baby sellers of Hickory Hill.

The trip had almost come to an end, when James and Robert saw the towering steel and glass of the John Hancock Building. The blinking red lights on its two towers were like beacons to the city dwellers. They were getting closer to home.

After a few days rest, the amateur detectives had their scheduled meeting with the authorities downtown. Everything went well. The couples had a good feeling about the case as they exited the Federal Building and headed for their favorite restaurant, Randalini's.

James requested their usual table next to the window overlooking the city and the lake. The friends were in a festive mood. The men treated the wives to their favorite meals. Life was back on track once again!

It was a clear afternoon. The sun glistened on the water of Lake Michigan. For a moment, James was reminded of the lacy shadows he had seen dance on the floor of the old house. The clinking of silverware on a glass and the sound of Robert's voice nudged him back to the reality of the conversation. "I would like to make a toast to our getaway adventure, our detective work, and, most of all, to the wonder of LIFE!" Robert said poetically.

"Now, who is the philosophical one?" chuckled James.

Robert continued, "In case you didn't notice, my lovely wife is not having her usual glass of wine, which she loves, with her favorite meal at Randalini's."

357

"Yes, yes, we noticed! So go on," James urged his best friend to continue.

Robert turned to Pat and encouraged, "Oh, honey, why don't you finish."

Pat began to cry tears of joy in front of her husband and best friends. "Robert and I have some good news to share with you—the best news we could have. We're going to have a baby!" she finally blurted out. The people sitting nearby in the restaurant smiled broadly and nodded kindly. "Our prayers have been answered. I didn't think it was going to happen for us, but it has!"

After the announcement from the expectant mother, James and Shelli were ecstatic about their best friends' wonderful news. There was much to celebrate on this sunny late afternoon in Chicago. Shelli leaned over toward her dearest friend and quizzed, "When did you go to the doctor, and when is the baby due?"

"Oh, I have been getting sick for the last few weeks. I thought it was the stress of all that 'detective' work stuff, you know, thinking about what we were going to have to do about the baby, the girl, Carla, and Nick. I just knew it was worry and anxiety. I tried to dismiss it while we were at Hickory Hill. I haven't been better since we returned, so I made an appointment with my primary care physician yesterday. He felt I should see my OB-GYN today before the meeting. She confirmed his suspicion. She said, 'Pat, you are PREGNANT!'"

The girls couldn't contain their excitement as they began to hug each other. The guys smiled as their wives embraced. James questioned, "OK, Pat, when is your due date?"

"The doctor said I am about twelve weeks pregnant—so about December 12."

James quickly calculated the weeks and months. Had Pat and Robert's baby been conceived at Crenshaw House?

Made in the USA
Lexington, KY
06 August 2017